Erle Stanley Gardner's
THE CASE OF THE MURDERER'S BRIDE
and Other Stories

Erle Stanley Gardner's
THE CASE OF THE MURDERER'S BRIDE
and Other Stories

Edited and with an Introduction by

ELLERY QUEEN

DAVIS PUBLICATIONS, INC.
229 Park Avenue South
New York, N.Y. 10003

The Editor hereby makes grateful acknowledgment to Thayer
Hobson and Company and to Lawrence Hughes for giving permission to reprint the material in this volume and for their generous
cooperation.

The Case of the Murderer's Bride, © 1957 by Erle Stanley Gardner.

The Candy Kid, copyright 1931 by Red Star News Co., copyright
renewed by Erle Stanley Gardner.

To Strike a Match (The House of Three Candles), copyright 1938
by Erle Stanley Gardner, renewed.

Death Rides a Boxcar, copyright 1944 by Erle Stanley Gardner,
renewed.

The Jeweled Butterfly, copyright 1952 by Erle Stanley Gardner.

CONTENTS

ERLE STANLEY GARDNER
An Unorthodox Introduction

biographical data]

Name: Erle Stanley Gardner. Born in Malden, Massachusetts, on July 17, 1889. Admitted to the California bar in 1911. Died on March 11, 1970. After the death of his first wife, married on August 7, 1968, to the woman who had been his Executive Secretary for many years—Jean Bethell. One child by his first marriage, Grace Naso.

publishing history]

Erle Stanley Gardner's first magazine story, "The Police of the House," was published in 1921. His first book was a Perry Mason novel, THE CASE OF THE VELVET CLAWS, published in 1933. [As of 1970, thirty-seven years after VELVET CLAWS, Mr. Gardner had written 143 books, of which 82 are Perry Mason titles and 15 are nonfiction.] No other author in the United States has equaled his total sales. The last compilation gave sales in the United States and Canada alone as approximately 200,000,000 copies.

working day, early in career]

He always had vivid recollections of putting in day after day trying a case in front of a jury, which is one of the most exhausting activities, then dashing up to the law library after court had adjourned to spend three or four hours looking up law points with which [Perry Mason-like] he could trip his adversary the next day, then going home, grabbing a glass of milk with an egg in it, dashing upstairs to his study, ripping the cover off his typewriter, noticing it was 11:30 p.m., and settling down with grim determination to get a plot for a story. Along about 3:00 in the morning he would have completed his daily stint of a 4000-word minimum and would crawl into bed, only to wake up about 5:00 with a new idea which he would transmit to the typewriter, then grab a hurried breakfast, shave and be on his way to the office where he'd rush through correspondence and dictation so he could beat it up to the courthouse and be on hand to smile at the jury promptly at 10:00. . . .During nearly all this time he had a schedule of having a novelette in the mail every third day, a schedule which he rigorously maintained.

[looking back on early-career working day]

Why the heck does a guy live like that? Mr. Gardner didn't know. He certainly didn't do it for money. About half of his law practice was given away, fighting for people who didn't have any money but whose rights had been infringed. . . . When he came right down to it, Mr. Gardner guessed it was just an inherent desire to accomplish a lot, realizing that life was going to be too short to do it.

[some personal characteristics]

He couldn't stand petty squabbles. He hated paper work. He didn't have the time to bicker about details. He went in for adventure, horseback riding, travel, and photography.

[sources of material; opinions; modus operandi]

He drew on his wealth of experience in the solution of crime. He also had 25 years of experience as a practicing trial lawyer.

He believed that readers like mystery stories because the story presents a problem which absorbs the attention of the reader and then brings that problem to a logical and final solution. Most readers are beset with a lot of problems they can't solve. When they try to relax, their minds keep gnawing over these problems and there is no solution. They pick up a mystery story, become completely absorbed in the problem, see the problem worked out to a final and just conclusion, turn out the light and go to sleep.

Few writers, he believed, analyze their methods of working out plots. He always did. To begin with, every story plot must have the lowest common denominator of public interest—the Cinderella basis, for example, used so often in Hollywood. . . . Mr. Gardner had quite a list of basic plots, but they were his secret—let the other boys figure out their own.

He thought modern detective stories far ahead of the earlier stories, so far as technique was concerned.

How long did it take him to write a novel? Thirty years ago he dictated a book in a week or ten days, revised and polished it and got it into the hands of the publisher within two or three weeks of the time he started. Later he revised and re-revised, and did so much reading that whenever he got a chance to relax he threw a saddle on a horse, picked up a gun or a bow and arrow, or climbed in a car and went tearing out in search of new material and adventure.

[*number of series characters*]

He always had a yen for series characters, but he didn't know how many he created. For some ten years prior to the publication of his first book, he wrote over 1,000,000 words a year which were sold to magazines. Back in the old wood-pulp days there was Senor Arnaz de Lobo, professional soldier of fortune and revolutionist; Jax Bowman (he couldn't remember anything about him!); Sidney Zoom and his police dog; the Patent Leather Kid, a suave, sinister chap; the firm of Small, Weston & Burke; Ed Jenkins, the Phantom Crook, a lone wolf type who ran in magazines for something over 20 years; Whispering Sands; Speed Dash, a human fly who developed a photographic memory—Mr. Gardner's first series character; Major Brane, free-lance secret service man; El Paisano, who could see in the dark; Larkin, a juggler who carried no other weapon than a billiard cue; Black Barr, a typical Western two-gun guy, who felt he was an instrument of divine justice; Hard Rock Hogan; Fong Dei; Crowder, Rapp; Skarle . . . [to say nothing of D.A. Douglas Selby; Bertha Cool and Donald Lam; Gramps Wiggins; Sheriff Bill Eldon; Terry Clane; Lester Leith; and, of course, the one and only Perry Mason].

[*number of pen names*]

A. A. Fair, Charles M. Green [his first], Kyle Corning, Grant Holiday, Robert Parr, Carleton Kendrake, Charles J. Kenny, Arthur Mann Sellers, Les Tillray, Dane Rigley, Charles M. Stanton.

[*the man behind the writer*]

For many years he investigated cases of innocent persons who had been wrongfully convicted, and, as a leading member of the so-called Court of Last Resort, he and several associates donated their time and at their own expense brought about ultimate justice in dozens of cases.

An Unorthodox Postscript

Dear Reader:

Now, just what is unorthodox about the preceding Introduction? Its form or arrangement? Yes. The impression that its components are somewhat disjointed, perhaps lacking in the smooth flow usually found in an editorial foreword? Yes. But there is something else—something far more unorthodox.

You had every right to assume that the Introduction you have just read was written by Ellery Queen. The front cover, the title page, the contents page all said so. Well, it is true that Ellery Queen wrote the longhand notes for the Introduction, organized the sequence of the notes, typed the first draft and the final copy, sent the text to the press for typesetting, proofread the galleys, and later the page proofs—but Ellery Queen did not *write* the Introduction.

A contradiction? Let us explain. When we persuaded Erle Stanley Gardner to permit us to publish his first book of short stories and novelettes—thus launching the Ellery Queen Presents series of original paperbacks—it was our intention to write an appreciative Introduction to Mr. Gardner and his work. But when we reread Erle's personal letters to your Editor over the years, and some of Erle's published reminiscences, we realized that the Introduction we had in mind had already been written—*by Erle Stanley Gardner himself!* And we realized further that we could not possibly write an Introduction as authentic and accurate as one entirely composed of statements written by Erle Stanley Gardner himself.

So the Introduction preceding this editorial postscript is most unorthodox because it could have been completely enclosed by quotation marks. With the exception of the words in [brackets] and such necessary but unimportant changes as substituting *Mr. Gardner* and *he* for *I*, and *his* for *my*, and changing to the past tense because of Mr. Gardner's death, every word, phrase, clause, and sentence came directly from the person who knew more about Erle Stanley Gardner and his career and work than anyone else in the world—the author himself.

So, let us end as we began—by quoting Mr. Gardner again. In the summer of 1951 we wrote to Erle and asked him, in connection with awards to be made later that year by *Ellery Queen's Mystery Magazine*, to nominate the ten best active mystery writers. On August 7, 1951, Erle replied with a long letter in which he explained why he could not nominate the ten best. His letter closed as follows (and finally we use quotation marks): ". . . if I should select a list of ten people whom I considered the best mystery writers, I would always be haunted by the feeling that I had done an injustice to the eleventh, twelfth, fifteenth, and seventy-fifth."

Now that, dear reader, tells more about Erle Stanley Gardner, about his sensitivity and conscientiousness and deep-rooted sense of fair play, than any biographical sketch or even any critical appraisal—not about Erle Stanley Gardner the best-selling American mystery writer of all time, but about Erle Stanley Gardner the man, the human being.

ELLERY QUEEN

THE CASE OF THE MURDERER'S BRIDE

L awrence B. Ives had two basic objections to the income tax. He objected to listing his occupation and he was annoyed that his business expenses could never be claimed as a deduction.

Lawrence B. Ives was in the business of murdering women.

So far as Ives was concerned, it was a reasonably safe and highly profitable occupation. It required a certain amount of research work, quite a bit of ingenuity, a pleasing personality, and a lot of reading.

Ives read the newspapers. He read them carefully, concentrating on news of tragic accidents.

Like many of our higher courts, Ives believed in following precedent. One tragic accident would arouse his interest. A duplication of that accident would start a file on the subject. A third such accident would cause him to start looking for a new wife. The fourth accident would then cause him to set his plan in motion.

New wives were not as difficult to find as the accidents.

Lawrence B. Ives never ceased to be astounded at the number of women who had passed the first third of their lives in a dull routine, who were starved for affection, and who had carefully saved their earnings.

His wives were all of a general type: women who had sacrificed their chances for early romance because of an unselfish devotion to family. After the sisters and brothers had married and the parents had passed away, these self-effacing breadwinners learned to accept vicarious love affairs. Being starved for affection, they frequented the newsstands, buying magazines which dealt with romance, or they spent long evenings in the public libraries.

Larry Ives was 36 years old, but he represented his age as a youthful 48. He spent considerable time and quite a bit of money buying his clothes. He was a good conversationalist and had a way of worming information out of librarians and from the clerks who presided over magazine counters. He also spent quite a bit of his time riding in public conveyances, looking for women who were reading the love-story type of magazine.

In making applications for a marriage license, he never listed his prior matrimonial adventures; but that was a minor omission—one which he regarded as of no greater legal importance than driving 50 miles an hour in a 35-mile zone. He could never be prosecuted for bigamy since, whenever Larry took on a new love, he was always definitely finished with the old. In fact, he made certain that his wives were very, very dead before moving on to his next conquest.

Earlier in his career, Larry had had to work with considerable rapidity. This had caused him to take certain risks. Now, with a large measure of financial stability, thanks to his unique gainful occupation, he didn't need to work so fast.

His current wife had been named Nan Palmer before she became the radiantly happy Mrs. Lawrence B. Ives.

Nan Palmer's outstanding characteristic had been family loyalty. She had had an unselfish devotion to those she loved. Her father had died when she was 12. By the time she was 16 she was supporting her mother, her sister Effie, and a younger brother.

Effie had selfish charm and dazzling beauty and was always promising the family a wealth of luxuries after she had "made good in Hollywood." She won a beauty contest when she was 18, and two divorces later had quit writing home.

Nan had put the younger brother through two years of college, and then he was killed in Korea. Her mother had never been strong enough to work, but had lingered on for years.

Nan's salary had been good, but it had all gone for living expenses, the ever-present doctor bills and nursing fees. There had been less and less money for Nan to spend on herself. She had learned to make her own clothes, she never went to a beauty shop, and she had adapted her life to a steady routine of drudgery: eight hours at the office, a ride home in a crowded bus during the rush hour, shopping at the market, cooking for an invalid, washing the dishes, cleaning up the house, doing the washing and ironing, sewing clothes, falling into bed, getting up in the morning to the chore of getting breakfast, washing the dishes, making the beds, and leaving for the office.

After Mrs. Palmer died, Nan had become so immersed in her routine that she didn't know what to do with her leisure. She had never before had leisure. Now she had time to read and she was thrilled by the adventures of heroines who were swept off their feet by gallant Prince Charmings who were always tall, generous, wavy-haired, thoughtful, handsome and wealthy.

Nan Palmer was made-to-order for Lawrence B. Ives.

At first she couldn't believe her senses. It seemed absolutely incredible when, after several chance meetings and brief conversations in the library, it became quite evident that Mr. Ives found her attractive.

Ives had his line down pat. He was, he said, a lonely widower who had traveled around the world. He wanted intellectual as well as physical companionship. He had learned that all is not gold that glitters and that beneath many a plain exterior there beats a warm, affectionate heart which is capable not only of steady affection but which can at times pour forth streams of molten passion. They were married in Yuma, Arizona.

Once having snared his victim into matrimony, it was a part of Ives's campaign to stress his wealth and his exciting plans for their future together. He disapproved of his wife's friends. He wanted to get her away from everything pertaining to her drab past.

None of his requests seemed odd to Nan. She was more than willing to escape from the colorless life she had always lived. She cooperated wholeheartedly by investing his money in beauty treatments, in charm and posture lessons, and in a sizable wardrobe of new clothes. Larry's wife, Nan reasoned, must be groomed to entertain as an attractive and charming hostess. She even took foreign-language courses so that she would be a credit to him when they went abroad. To Nan, life had just begun, and she planned to live it in the fullest possible manner.

The drain on Larry's capital caused him some dismay. It seemed a rather unnecessary expenditure on a woman who would be laid to rest in a few months. But the results, he had to admit, were esthetically satisfying. He was astounded at the change in the woman who had been drab Nan Palmer. She had continued to wear her dark hair in a manner which best suited her simplicity. Her figure became strikingly attractive, and her taste in clothes proved to be unerringly chic—as well as consistently expensive.

Her first bashful responses to love had suddenly been swept along on a tide of released emotion until Ives found himself thinking of "retiring" and settling down to enjoy himself with his loving wife.

However, the chains of habit are strong. Sooner or later a man always returns to what the police list in their files as *modus operandi*. And so there came the day when Ives brought up the matter of life insurance.

Ives didn't care for large policies. He preferred small policies with different companies, and he knew of several companies which wrote insurance by mail. In fact, Ives had a most comprehensive knowledge of life insurance. His wife saw nothing suspicious about this. Her husband had a brilliant mind and a dazzling fund of general information.

After nine months of marriage Nan still couldn't believe her good fortune. She would sit by the hour while Larry was scanning the newspapers, watching him with her heart in her eyes. He was wonderful.

Ives, despite himself, followed his habit of scanning the papers, although somewhat reluctantly. In the past he had always been impatient as he built up his file of unusual but fatal accidents. Now, when he would gladly have taken a more leisurely course, it seemed that suitable accidents were described in every issue of the newspapers.

One class of fatal accident, however, claimed Ives's attention with a certain fascination. These accidents were capable of artistic developments which thrilled the creative urge in his soul.

Ives had three clippings on these: one had occurred on Lake Mead, another on Lake Tahoe, and the third on Lake Edward, The fatalities were such as to lend themselves admirably to Ives's scheme. They were particularly suited to the place at which he had chosen to become a grieving widower.

People went out in boats with outboard motors. The weather was warm, the surface of the lake was flat calm. They stopped the motors and drifted along far out from shore. The urge to jump in for a cooling dip where they needed no bathing suits became irresistible. So over the side they went.

Though the lake was calm, there was a gentle breeze. The weather station placed it at two to five miles an hour. However, because the boat was drifting slowly along with that breeze, the boaters didn't notice it. It wasn't until they had been swimming for a minute or two that they turned their attention to the boat. They saw it some 200 yards away. Startled, they started swimming toward the boat.

Panic led them to assume a pace they couldn't maintain. For a while they were gaining; then they slowed down in breathless fatigue. The boat glided in effortless mockery, steadily moving, always out of reach. Again the swimmers, lured by the seeming nearness of the boat, spurted into frenzied swimming.

Unless they were unusually strong swimmers they could never make it. The boat would be drifting as fast or a little faster than they could swim. So they became panic-stricken.

By the time the most powerful swimmer in the group, who had worked himself into a state of almost complete exhaustion, finally decided to quit the futile pursuit of the drifting boat, at least one of his companions was missing. Once a swimmer reaches a point of complete exhaustion in fresh water, panic will do the rest.

Three accidents. Ives needed a fourth in order to make his scheme perfect.

He found it on page one of the second section of the paper:

DRIFTING BOAT CAUSES TRAGEDY ON HAVASU LAKE.

Larry looked over at his wife. For a long moment he hesitated; then he slipped a sharp penknife from his pocket and cut the clipping from the paper.

"What is it?" Nan asked.

"A report on some mining activities, dear. . . . How would you like to take our boat and trailer over to the Colorado River?"

"I'd *love* it, darling!"

Larry sighed and regarded her speculatively, almost wistfully. Then he tightened his lips with firm decision. After all, Ives was a businessman, and the premiums on those insurance policies, not to mention Nan's extravagances, amounted to a fairly heavy outlay.

It was the duty of Corporal Ed Cortland to read all the crank mail that came to the police department.

This mail was of all sorts: rambling dissertations from persons who felt they were being persecuted, anonymous tips from disgruntled neighbors, phony confessions from persons who had no real knowledge of the details of the crimes to which they were confessing. They had read newspaper accounts of some crime, and brooded over it, and finally had sought to make atonement for some real or fancied sin they had committed by confession to one they hadn't.

Corporal Cortland had a trained eye in such matters. He could spot the type of writer from a glance at the first paragraph.

The fifty-second letter that he opened on this May morning was different from the others. It read:

"I am writing to the police department because I don't know to whom else I can write.

"I knew Nan Palmer when she worked up here. She was steady, industrious, a quiet girl who gave the best years of her life to an invalid mother.

"Then Prince Charming came along. He gave the name of Lawrence B. Ives, and he really was handsome. None of could see why he was so attracted to Nan.

"It was a whirlwind courtship. They took a plane to
ıma and were married. Soon after that they moved away.
ıd Nan never wrote to any of her friends.

"I wouldn't have had any idea where she was living if it
dn't been that an insurance company wanted to find out
mething about her in connection with an insurance pol-
y she was taking out. The investigator talked with me.
: told me she was living somewhere in or near Los
ıgeles.

"I still thought nothing of it until I happened to be look-
g through an old illustrated magazine in cleaning out
me of the papers in my attic.

"I saw a man's picture and knew there was something
miliar about the face. At first I couldn't place it, then I
ddenly realized it was Lawrence B. Ives.

"Only this time he wasn't going under that name, but
der the name of Corvallis E. Fletcher.

"His picture had been published in connection with a
ıgic accident. He had gone up with his wife in a light
ıne and had persuaded the pilot to do a few stunts. Both
ıssengers had reported their safety belts were firmly fas-
ıed, but it turned out that Mrs. Fletcher hadn't under-
ıod the proper method of fastening her seat belt. She had
ın thrown out of the plane and had fallen 3,000 feet.

"As soon as I saw that picture I was certain I'd seen the
ın before. It isn't a very good picture and he had a mus-
:he at the time, but I feel certain it's the same man. I'm
ıding the picture along together with the clipping.

"I think the Fletcher accident should be checked, and I
ınk someone had better ask Mr. Ives how it happened he
ınged his name.

"This is just a hunch, and if you do anything about it, for
ıaven's sake don't let Nan know that I wrote this letter. I
ırked with her for several years, and I like her and she
ıd to like me. I don't want her to think I'm getting nosey
ıd interfering in her affairs."

Corporal Cortland put this letter to one side and during
 course of the evening mentioned it to his friend, Dr.
ırbert Dixon, the medico-legal expert on forensic pathol-

ogy and homicide investigation. Dr. Dixon became interested.

It took the police less than an hour to locate the apartment house where Mr. and Mrs. Ives lived. Dr. Dixon and Corporal Cortland drove around to the place. The manager, a large friendly woman named Mrs. Meehan, explained that Mr. and Mrs. Ives had left on a trip. They had given up the apartment and had loaded some of their baggage into their car; the balance had gone into storage. She understood they were going to live in Arizona. They had taken their boat, outboard motor, and trailer with them.

Mrs. Meehan informed them that Mr. Ives was a remarkable personality—charming, magnetic, polished. His wife was sweet and really beautiful. They were *very* happy together. Mr. Ives didn't work. He evidently had some sort of independent income. Mrs. Meehan thought he was interested in mining.

Mr. Ives had settled all their bills before they left. They had only been gone a couple of days and the apartment wasn't cleaned up yet. It would be put in shape tomorrow. Mrs. Meehan let Corporal Cortland into the apartment and left him and Dr. Dixon there to look around.

Dr. Dixon found the copy of the newspaper from which a news item had been cut out. The edges of the cut showed that it had been made with a sharp knife held by someone with a steady hand.

Corporal Cortland rang up the newspaper office, got them to check the issue in question and relay the story to him. When Dr. Dixon learned that it was a story of a tragic accident in which two swimmers had been lost in Lake Havasu, he became thoughtful.

A check of the telephone company showed that Ives had paid up his account. The record showed that the last long distance call on record was to Searchlight, Nevada.

When Dr. Dixon phoned the Nevada number, the man who answered remembered Ives's call well. The man operated a service station, and from his office he could relay calls over a private telephone line which stretched across the desert to Lee Bracket's Eldorado Landing, a distance of 50-odd miles by road.

Ives had asked him to relay a call through to Bracket's to see if accommodations were available, and the reservations had been made.

The service-station manager said that usually when he accommodated people by making reservations for them, they at least did him the courtesy of stopping in at his station to say thank you and to fill up their tanks with gasoline.

Ives had done neither.

After this conversation Dr. Dixon reached a quick decision. "I've been planning on a little vacation, Ed. I'm going to drive down there to the Colorado. Think you could get permission to go along?"

"I could if you recommended it as an investigative job," Corporal Cortland said, grinning.

"I'll recommend it." Dr. Dixon grinned back.

The road to Bracket's camp wound down a long slope from the crest of the mountains to the river. The last two or three miles ran past weird rock formations that looked like great petrified mushrooms.

Where the Colorado River had once been a turgid, dangerous stream, there was now a clear blue lake stretching from Davis Dam, some 40 miles to the south of Eldorado Wash, to Hoover Dam, 20 miles to the north.

"This," Corporal Cortland announced with conviction, "is the life."

They found Lee Bracket playing gin rummy with a tourist whose dour expression was an eloquent reflection of his mismatched cards.

Lee Bracket didn't discuss his guests with strangers, and Corporal Cortland, correctly interpreting Dr. Dixon's faint shake of the head, refrained from producing his credentials and making the visit official.

They did learn, however, that boats were available for daily rental. A survey of the parking facilities showed that a car bearing Ives's license number and an empty boat trailer were parked in position.

Guarded inquiries of the attendant in charge of the boat landing brought out the information that Ives and his wife were not fishing but were collecting rocks.

For miles around the camp the slopes were composed of riverworn sand-polished rocks of varying sizes. Even the rankest amateur could pick up beautifully colored agates, jasper, and fossil-encrusted rocks. Some of these could be cut into gem stones; others could be "tumbled" into colorful collections of costume jewelry.

The attendant at the dock described Ives's boat: a 15-footer, red and white, of glass fiber, powered by a 35-h.p. outboard motor, capable of some 25 miles per hour.

The only boat which was available for renting was considerably slower. Dr. Dixon and Cortland rented this boat and spent the rest of the day in a futile search, Dr. Dixon sweeping his binoculars in a study of every boat they encountered.

They returned to Bracket's just about dark to find Ives's boat tied up at the dock.

While Dr. Dixon stood guard, Corporal Cortland gave the boat a swift survey. A cardboard carton in the bottom contained 20 or 30 pounds of desert agates and jasper. Quite evidently, Mr. and Mrs. Ives had spent most of the day on shore gathering specimens.

In the camp's dining room Dixon and the police officer encountered Mr. and Mrs. Ives, as well as several other guests, in conversation around the large circular dinner table. The two men joined the group and without any indication of their professional pursuit they introduced themselves. They were welcomed with friendly informality.

Ives, Dr. Dixon noted, was somewhat reticent, but courteous and affable. Mrs. Ives was a beauty. Her conversation was brisk and intelligent and her sense of humor was as apparent as her happiness. Nor was there any doubt about her devotion to her husband.

Ives seemed quite solicitous about the weather. He asked repeated questions about the winds. It was clear that he had no intention of getting caught in a storm or rough weather.

"We are really landlubbers at heart," Mrs. Ives laughed. "You don't ever need worry about us," she assured the proprietor. "We only go out when it is pleasant."

Later that night Dr. Dixon discussed the matter with Corporal Cortland. "I've never seen a woman so bride-eyed. She is desperately in love with him, Ed. We can't afford to make a wrong move. Not only would we be exposing ourselves to a suit for damages and for defamation of character, but what would be even worse, we might be ruining her faith in her husband."

"But we have the goods on him," Cortland insisted. "We know he's been going under another name. It's the same guy all right."

Dr. Dixon said, "Suppose he *was* going under another name? It's only a suspicious circumstance, that's all. We're going to have to wait until headquarters gets some more information on this Corvallis E. Fletcher."

"Okay by me," Corporal Cortland said with a sudden grin. "This is the most pleasant assignment I've had in twenty years. Only let's not give him so much rope that he can be dangerous."

"We'll try to keep an eye on things," Dr. Dixon said. "We—"

He broke off as the door of one of the cabins opened and an oblong of bright light pierced the darkness. A figure was silhouetted against the oblong.

"That's Ives now," Cortland whispered.

Ives, apparently with something under his left arm, stepped out of the cottage, turned to say something over his shoulder, closed the door, and then, producing a small flashlight, started down the sloping road to the wharf landing.

Dr. Dixon tapped Cortland on the arm. The two followed silently, staying in the shadow of the cliff to the south of the road.

They heard Ives's steps on the boards of the wharf.

"He's putting something in," Dr. Dixon said. "We're in a precarious situation here, Ed. He might spot our reflections in the water. Let's get down and sit close, so we'll seem to be a shapeless shadow."

They sat on their heels.

"I'd like to go shake the guy down," Cortland grumbled.

"We can't take the chance, Ed—not until we can get a

definite identification on that picture. Even then, we've go
to find out something more about his background before w
dare to move in. I wouldn't make a mistake in this case fo
worlds. I keep thinking of that look of utter devotion in he
eyes! She's hypnotized. It would be a crime to spoil it."

They heard vague, muffled sounds from Ives's boat.

Soon I'ves's feet pounded back along the wooden whar
crunched on the gravel of the road, and then they saw hin
walking slowly back up the hill to his cabin. He seemed t
be carrying something in his right hand.

Dr. Dixon and Corporal Cortland fell in behind so the
could see his silhouette against the light from the cabi
grounds.

Midway to the cabins, Ives stopped at the garbag
disposal barrel and tossed something in. Then he walke
on to the cabin door. A moment later he was flooded wit
light from the interior of the cabin. The watchers saw
pair of arms circle his neck. Ives stepped inside, the doo
was closed, and it was dark once more.

"Now what the hell!" Cortland said. "He went down t
the boat for some purpose. Do you suppose he's suspiciou
of us and went down to see if we'd been examining th
boat?"

Dr. Dixon shook his head. "He didn't even look bac
when he went down to the boat or when he returned to th
cabin. He isn't suspicious—unless, of course, he's *very* su
picious and is laying a trap for us. The first thing we mus
do is to see what he tossed into that barrel."

They waited a half hour, then Corporal Cortland led th
way to the disposal barrel and played his flashlight on th
contents.

The big metal drum was three-quarters' full: empty ti
cans, cardboard cartons, a pair of discarded tennis shoes.

"It must have been the tennis shoes," Cortland said.

Dr. Dixon leaned over to study the barrel carefully.

"It has to be on top, Ed," he said. "He didn't bend ov
the barrel, as would have been necessary if he had shove
anything down. He just dropped something in. Moreover,
he had moved anything, these empty cans would ha
made a clatter."

24

"It *has* to be the tennis shoes," Cortland decided.

"Let's take an inventory," Dr. Dixon said. "There are a pork-and-beans can, a cereal carton, two dishwashing detergent boxes, a tomato-juice can; here are two empty sardine cans, a newspaper, the tennis shoes, a pair of badly bedraggled socks and . . . wait a minute, what's this? Here's a pair of pliers with one of the jaws broken off."

"It must have been the tennis shoes," Cortland said.

He picked them up. The shoes had been badly worn down to the point where the sole on the right shoe had a circle which had worn almost through.

"A tennis player," Cortland said. "He pivots on his right foot when he serves. Notice how the right shoe is worn more than the left."

Dr. Dixon remained thoughtfully silent.

"Not convinced?" Cortland asked.

"I don't want to jump to conclusions," Dr. Dixon said. "Let's go take a look inside that boat."

"Do you suppose he could have planted a bomb in the boat, one that's due to explode tomorrow sometime?"

"Anything's possible," Dr. Dixon said, "but we've got to have evidence before we make any move."

They searched the boat thoroughly. It contained a paddle, an anchor attached to 50 feet of new rope, a spare gasoline tank for the motor, and two kapok-filled cushions which could be used as life preservers in an emergency. There were no fishing rods, no bait boxes, nothing to indicate that the boat had ever been used except for hunting rocks. There was, however, a new icepick. There was no sign of anything that could have been used to conceal a bomb.

"He didn't put anything *in* the boat," Ed said at length. "He took something *out*."

"He had something with him when he went down to the boat," Dr. Dixon pointed out.

"The tennis shoes, Doctor?"

"Why should he take the tennis shoes down to the boat, stay in the boat a while, then turn around, bring the same tennis shoes back, and throw them away?"

"How do we know they're the *same* tennis shoes?" Cortland asked. "Suppose he bought a new pair of tennis shoes. He had left his old ones in the boat. He went down to the boat, put on his new tennis shoes, picked up the old tennis shoes, took them back and threw them away."

"Then these old tennis shoes had been left in the boat?" Dr. Dixon asked.

"Yes."

"He walked down to the boat carrying new tennis shoes with him, put on the new tennis shoes down here, and took the old tennis shoes back. That still leaves an extra pair of shoes. What happened to the shoes he was wearing when he walked down to the boat?"

Cortland thought that over. "I guess I'm getting ahead of myself, Doc," he admitted. "But I still think the tennis shoes are the key to the whole thing. Let's go back to the cabin and get to bed. We can't do any more here."

It was four o'clock in the morning when Nan Ives suddenly awoke. She lay still, her heart beating rapidly as though she had been startled. Then, as she felt the secure warmth of Larry's arms around her, she relaxed and sighed happily.

"Let's get up, darling," Larry whispered.

She turned toward him.

"Now? It's so early."

"It's wonderful out. The stars are blazing. It will be light by the time we get the boat going, and we can see the dawn out on the lake."

She smiled. "Just as you say, dearest," she said and kissed him.

While they were dressing she said, "What about breakfast?"

"That," he said, "is the nice part of it. We'll go down to Cottonwood Cove for breakfast. The scenery is beautiful on the way down there and they have a nice little restaurant with good cooking. You'll love it."

Fifteen minutes later, arm in arm, they were walking down the sloping roadway toward the water.

The east was beginning to show light. Already a slight tinge of color brightened the sky. Overhead and to the west, however, the stars were steady, blazing, and brilliant; the air was warm and balmy. The water was like a sheet of glass, reflecting the eastern sky, the stars, and the dark outlines of the mountains which bordered the lake.

Larry helped his wife into the boat, saw that she was comfortably ensconced on a seat cushion, and, having untied the boat, pushed off into the warm half-darkness.

Dr. Herbert Dixon, awakening early, showered, dressed, and returned to the bedroom where Corporal Ed Cortland was sleeping soundly.

The criminologist stood over Cortland with a wet washcloth in his hand and squeezed a single drop of cold water on Cortland's forehead.

The officer twisted his face in an expression of distaste. A second drop caused him to sit up, throwing off the covers.

"Hey!" he said thickly.

Dr. Dixon grinned. "Come on, up and at 'em, boy! This is a new day."

"What time is it?"

"Six o'clock."

"Go away, that's too early. No need to get up yet. We can't even get any coffee. The people that run this place don't stay here; they live seven miles up the road."

"Never mind coffee," Dr. Dixon said. "We'll reconnoiter. Perhaps we can have a chance to talk with Ives before breakfast."

"Slave driver," Cortland groaned, getting out of bed.

Dr. Dixon plugged in his electric shaver and by the time Cortland was half through with his shower, the criminologist was walking slowly down the road to the water.

He moved toward the dock, then suddenly stiffened to attention, whirled, and started walking rapidly back up the hill to the cabins.

"Hey, Ed," he said, "Ives's boat is gone."

"You kidding?" Cortland asked.

"No. It's not there."

"What about the automobile and the trailer?"

"They're here."

"Then they must have taken off for some rock hunting. They'll be back for breakfast."

Dr. Dixon frowned. "Hang it!" he said. "Perhaps Ives did suspect us. If anything happens. . . . Well, it'll be just too bad for him."

"Don't be too sure," Cortland said pessimistically. "You have to have proof, remember? And the trouble with accidents is that the survivor always tells a plausible story; he's the only witness and—"

"Come on," Dr. Dixon interrupted, "let's go."

"Upstream or down?"

"We start upstream," Dr. Dixon said. "They were downstream yesterday. They've probably gone up today."

"We can't get breakfast anywhere up there."

"Yes, we can. Willow Beach. Twelve miles or so. We can be having hot coffee in an hour if you'll just get started."

They made the run up to Willow Beach. They saw majestic scenery, towering vertical cliffs reflected in placid water, the golden line of sunlight crawling slowly down the mountains. But there was no sign of Mr. and Mrs. Ives.

At Willow Beach they stopped for a fast breakfast and talked with a fisherman who had been out early and who said no boat had gone by.

Hurrying from the restaurant, they gassed up, opened the motor wide, and headed downriver. They gassed again at Bracket's. By this time the sunlight was warm. The lake seemed calm, but looking along the reflected path of the sun one could see the glint of small ripples.

Corporal Cortland was running the motor. Dr. Dixon was carefully scanning the lake with the binoculars, frowning impatiently at the numerous coves in which a small craft might find concealment. Dr. Dixon felt he didn't have the time to go into each one of those coves. A sixth sense gave him a feeling of urgency.

He wanted desperately to catch sight of Ives's boat. Something seemed to tell him that this was the crucial day. It was exactly the sort of day that had been described in the newspaper clipping—warm with a faint breeze and the urge to swim becoming more and more a temptation.

Both above and below Bracket's camp a rough attempt

had been made to designate the miles by painting figures in white on rocks along the shore, or by arranging whitewashed rocks in the form of figures.

At seven miles below the landing Ed Cortland mistook the channel and went into a big bay, which finally curved back to disclose the true channel. Going around a point they came to where the lake broadened out into a vast sheet of water.

Now, from time to time, they saw other small boats. This caused more loss of time. Dr. Dixon had to study each boat with binoculars. Nor did he dare stop passers-by to give them a description of Ives's boat and to ask if they had seen it. He did not want Ives to know that he was taking an unusual interest in him.

After the nine-mile sign Dr. Dixon found no more signs. There was, he felt, a ten-mile sign, but somewhere he had missed it. A growing tension developed inside him.

He moved aft to sit beside Ed Cortland at the tiller.

"Ed," he said, "I've thought of something."

"What?"

"The thing that happened last night. We looked into that trash barrel and—"

"And saw those tennis shoes," Cortland reminded him.

"That's what fooled us," Dr. Dixon said. "Everything else that was in there was something you would have *expected* to find in a disposal unit out in front of cabins. The tennis shoes were unusual, so they attracted attention. Everything else was perfectly ordinary, except perhaps the broken pliers."

"What are you getting at?" Cortland asked.

"Ives threw something in there," Dr. Dixon said. "We thought it might have been the tennis shoes because they were unusual, but we can't make his action in doing that sound logical because he carried something down with him under his left arm, and when he came back he dropped something in the barrel." He paused. "There were two empty detergent boxes in it."

"But what would a detergent have to do with murder?"

Dr. Dixon indicated the cushion on which he was seated. "The Coast Guard requires life preservers in a boat," he said. "These cushions are filled with kapok. They act in the dual capacity of seat cushions and life preservers. The kapok is exceedingly light and it's oil- and water-resistant. It's buoyant, not only because of its own lightness, but because the oily surface repels the water and holds lots of air bubbles trapped inside the matted interior of the light, fluffy substance.

"Now, then, a detergent is a peculiar chemical compound. It consists of a substance which has an affinity both for oil and for water. It's as though you had a long molecule, one end of which is fastened to the oil, the other end fastened to the water."

"What are you getting at?"

"Put enough powdered detergent inside one of these seat cushions and throw it in the water," Dr. Dixon continued, "and for a while nothing will happen. The outer surface is water-repellent, but as soon as water starts getting in, it will mingle with the powdered detergent and then more water will start getting in. The minute the powdered detergent mingles with the water, it becomes a wetting agent and the cushion will rapidly lose its buoyancy.

"When detergents were first invented, they conducted an experiment by putting a duck in the water to which a detergent had been added. The wetting agent caused the oily feathers of the duck to attract water; the duck sank to the bottom of the tank and would have drowned if they hadn't taken it out."

Ed Cortland looked at Dr. Dixon. "Then you think that Ives—"

"I think," Dr. Dixon said, "that Lawrence Ives might have gone down to his boat, cut small openings in those kapok cushions, and filled both of them with powdered detergent. Then he might have punched holes in the covers with that icepick and put small pieces of tape over the cuts to keep the kapok from working out. In the event of an 'accident,' they would have to rely on the life preservers. And if Mrs. Ives can't swim. . . ."

Dr. Dixon left the sentence significantly unfinished.

"Good heavens!" Cortland said. "That clipping was about a swimming accident."

Dr. Dixon nodded. "Exactly. Suppose you were going swimming where you expected an accident to take place. Where would you go?"

"What do you mean?"

"Not out here in the main channel where a fishing boat might come by in time to perform a spectacular rescue. You'd go out where you would have privacy. Remember when we came around that stretch, we left a long sweep of water behind us back from the main channel. It's just a hunch, Ed, and time is running out—"

Corporal Ed Cortland swung the boat in a sharp turn.

Lawrence Ives stopped the motor of the boat and smiled at his wife. "This is so beautiful, darling," he said, "let's just sit here and admire the scenery."

Slowly the boat lost headway until the waves of the churning wake became gentle ripples; then the placid calm of the lake surrounded them.

"Not quite calm enough for the reflections to be clear," Ives said, "but the air is still and beautiful."

They sat in silence for a while, and then Nan slipped her hand confidingly into Larry's. "I'm so completely happy," she said. "I never knew what a difference being in love could make."

"Neither did I," Larry said absently.

The minutes passed. Each was absorbed with thoughts. Nan was soaking in the beauties, basking in the warmth. Larry was carefully studying the lake, the shoreline, and the almost imperceptible drift.

He lit a cigarette and tossed the match overboard. The distance between the match and the boat widened, despite the fact that the boat seemed to remain stationary. It was as though some mysterious force had started moving the match away from the boat.

"Let's take a swim," Ives suggested suddenly.

"We didn't bring our suits," Nan protested.

"Out here, we don't need them," Ives said. "Let's jump in and—"

"But, Larry, I don't swim very well."

"I know you don't, but you don't need to," he assured her.

"We'll take our cushions along. They're life preservers, you know. There's no one out here to see us. Look at that water. Isn't it irresistible?"

It took only a little more persuasion; then she slipped out of her clothes and went over the side.

Ives tossed her a cushion from the rear seat, stripped, took the other cushion, and jumped overboard.

They splashed about in the water as gaily as children.

Ives surreptitiously watched the boat. It was drifting just as he had expected. Now he was in a foolproof position. If some boat came along and rescued them, they could tell the story of an ordinary boating mishap. No significance would ever be attached to it. If, on the other hand, no boat came along. . . . In a short time Lawrence B. Ives would be ready once more to enjoy a period of complete freedom and relaxation.

Oddly enough, the thought of being free again did not excite him so much as it had on previous similar occasions. As he had watched Nan slip into the water, there had been a sharp stab of reluctance at the thought of losing her. It was not a pang of conscience; Lawrence Ives had no conscience. It was just that he realized that what Nan had said about being in love was true.

With a self-discipline that came from rigid training, he turned his mind to the insurance, and to the thoughts of the luxury and the variety it would afford him. It was at that moment that Nan noticed the boat.

"Look how far we've come, Larry," she cried.

"Good heavens!" Ives said. "*We* haven't moved! It's the boat that's drifting! There must be a wind. Stay right here and cling to the cushion, darling. Hold it tight against you. I'm going after the boat."

"Can you catch it?" she asked.

"I think so," he assured her. "I'll put my cushion under my chest and swim. I think I can make it. In any event, the cushion will keep me afloat and you'll be perfectly safe waiting right here. I'll get the boat and bring it back."

He swam away without once looking back.

Cortland piloted their boat back to the bend in the river.

"Now veer off to the left. Let's try that broad expanse up there," Dr. Dixon suggested. He moved up to the bow to study the situation with his glasses.

Suddenly he called, "Over there to the right, Ed. That looks like Ives's boat."

"I can't see it," Ed shouted above the roar of the motor.

"It's off to the right. You can't see it without the glasses. Move over a little. Steady. There you are. Hold it right on this course."

Dr. Dixon braced himself, holding the binoculars to his eyes. The boat surged ahead, making only fair speed with its small motor.

After a while Cortland shouted, "I can see it now, Doc. What do you make out?"

Dr. Dixon was silent for a moment; then he moved back to where Cortland was at the motor. "There's no one in it, Ed," he said grimly. "It's drifting with the slight breeze, but I can't see anyone."

Corporal Cortland's lips tightened. "When that guy tells his story it had better be *good*," he muttered.

Dr. Dixon began turning his head, sweeping the binoculars across the water. Suddenly he reached over to grasp Cortland's arm.

"Turn it back to the left, Ed. Someone's in the water."

"Where?"

"Swing it around! Over to the left. . . . Not quite so far. Keep going."

A little over three minutes later, Ed slowed the boat next to the head and shoulders of Mrs. Lawrence B. Ives.

"You need help?" Dr. Dixon called.

"Yes, yes. Oh, please help him," she sobbed. "My husband, my husband!"

"Come on aboard. Here, let me give you a hand," Dr. Dixon said.

"I'm . . . I have no suit. . . ."

"I'm a doctor," Dixon reassured her. "We have a coat you can put around you. Come on."

They helped her aboard and Dr. Dixon covered her with a coat.

"What happened?" Dr. Dixon asked.

Her eyes were dark with panic.

"Larry," she said. "My husband. Oh, you must find him! You must! He's in the lake near here somewhere. He took off after our boat, and then I heard him calling and calling and then I didn't hear him any more. I tried to push my cushion through the water, but—"

"Take it easy now, take it easy," Corporal Cortland said. "Tell us exactly what happened."

"We stopped the boat and went swimming, and there was a current or a wind or something, and the boat started drifting. I'm not a good swimmer. Larry isn't a *strong* swimmer, but he thought he could take after the boat. He told me to hang onto my life preserver and not let go of it no matter what happened."

Dr. Dixon and Corporal Cortland exchanged glances.

First, they went to the empty boat. Dr. Dixon picked up Nan Ives's clothes. The men turned their backs while she dressed. Then they started combing the water carefully, covering every inch. They retrieved the kapok cushion to which the woman had been clinging. There was no sign of the other cushion.

And there was no sign of Lawrence B. Ives.

They searched for two hours before they reluctantly admitted defeat. Dr. Dixon, with the painstaking attention to detail of a trained criminologist, had made cross-bearings showing the exact location of the tragedy. With Ives's boat in tow, they headed toward Cottonwood Cove.

Mrs. Ives was inconsolable. "Why, oh, why did that have to happen to us?" she said. "We were so happy, so wonderfully, deliriously happy; and now—"

Again Dr. Dixon exchanged significant glances with Cortland.

"Just bear up, ma'am," the Corporal said. "It's tough, all right, but time heals all wounds."

At Cottonwood Cove they organized a searching party. The wife of one of the owners fixed Nan Ives up in a chair on the cool porch of the luxurious floating dock. Dr. Dixon sat with her for a while, talking quietly, consoling her.

He and Corporal Cortland held a brief conference before

going out to join the searching party.

"Get this straight, Ed," Dr. Dixon said. "She's never to know about any of this. Let her have the memory of a perfect marriage."

"Who do you think is going to tell her?" Dr. Dixon admitted.

"I'm not *that* dumb," Cortland protested. "It's better for her to spend the rest of her life being true to the memory of one of nature's noblemen than to go back to being a wallflower."

Dr. Dixon laughed. "She may have been a wallflower when Ives married her, but she has turned into an orchid now. With a face and figure like hers it won't be long before a string of eligible males will be trying to make her forget the tragedy that made her a wealthy widow."

"Wealthy?" Cortland repeated, and his eyebrows raised.

Dr. Dixon nodded. "Mrs. Ives mentioned that she and her husband had joint insurance policies and joint bank accounts—all payable to the survivor. It was her idea, not that she ever thought of personal gain. She wanted them for the protection of their future children."

Dr. Dixon shook his head. "She seems to have outwitted him all around. But what puzzles me is how Ives happened to grab the wrong life preserver. Evidently, he put detergent in only one cushion. How the devil did he make the mistake?"

He frowned suddenly. "Do you suppose *she* could have switched the cushions?"

Cortland shook his head. "I did," he admitted. "When we were down looking over the boat last night."

Dr. Dixon stared at him. "Do you mean to say you *knew* what Ives had in mind?"

"Hell, no," Cortland confessed. "I just swapped those cushions around as a matter of principle. Just good old police routine. I knew we were dealing with a crook and I acted automatically. It is an axiom of police procedure—never let a crook leave a setup!"

LESTER LEITH versus SERGEANT ACKLEY in

THE CANDY KID

Lester Leith, slender, debonair, gathered the lounging robe about him and sprawled at silken ease.

"Scuttle, the cigarettes."

His valet proffered the case of monogrammed cigarettes with a synthetic servility which ill became the massive hulk of the man.

"Yes, sir," he said.

"And the crime clippings. I think I'd like to read about crime."

The valet, who was in reality no valet at all, but a policy spy employed to watch Lester Leith and report his every move, let his thick lips twist into a grin.

"Yes, sir. I was going to speak to you about them. Your prediction has come true."

"My prediction, Scuttle?"

"Yes, sir. You remember Carter Mills, the gem expert?"

Lester Leith puckered his forehead.

"Mills . . . The name seems to be familiar, Scuttle. . . . Oh, yes, he was the one who was working on the ruby necklace for some rajah or other. He insisted on grabbing all the newspaper publicity he could get. I remember the headline: Carries a Million Dollars to Work."

The valet nodded. "Yes, sir. That's the one. You remember he had his photograph taken with a leather brief case in his hand. The newspaper article mentioned that he carried a fortune in rare gems back and forth from his place of business to his house. He was making a design for the rubies, flanked with diamonds. It was to be something unique in the art of gem setting, sir, and—"

"Yes, yes, Scuttle. There's no need to go into it again, but you'll remember that I mentioned he was simply inviting danger."

"Yes, sir. You said that Mr. Mills didn't realize how businesslike the underworld had become. You mentioned that he would find himself robbed someday and that his client would find, to his grief, that it didn't pay to have a gem designer who carried a million dollars' worth of stones around in a brief case."

Leith nodded. "I take it, Scuttle, that all this is merely a preface to telling me that Mr. Mills *was* robbed?"

"Yes, sir. Yesterday morning, sir. He went to work in a taxicab. He was carrying the brief case stuffed with gems and sketches. When he opened his shop he found a man standing inside with a gun. The man ordered Mills to come in and lock the door, and Mills had to obey. The man took the brief case and started to run for the back.

"But Mills hadn't been altogether foolish. He had installed a burglar alarm just inside the door, and he'd notified the occupants of adjoining buildings what it would mean when the burglar alarm sounded.

"He pressed the burglar alarm and then grabbed a shotgun which he kept behind the counter for just such an emergency. He fired, and he fired low. Some of the pellets hit the bandit's legs.

"The sound of the shots and the noise of the burglar alarm made a terrific commotion. You see, it was early in the morning. Mr. Mills makes a habit of being the first one to come to his shop every morning. I believe it was about ten minutes to eight, sir.

"But there were clerks in some of the adjoining stores, and there was a traffic officer on duty at the corner. Naturally, these men all got into action.

"By the time the bandit reached the alley there were two clerks waiting for him. He ran toward a car that was parked in the alley and started it. But the clerks shouted to the traffic officer and he sprinted for the mouth of the alley.

"The bandit saw him coming, jumped out of the car, still carrying the brief case, and dashed into the rear door of a candy store."

Lester Leith held up his hand.

"Just a moment, Scuttle. You say he was wounded, this bandit?"

"Yes, sir."

"Bleeding, Scuttle?"

"Yes, sir."

"Clerks behind him raising an alarm?"

"Yes, sir, and Mr. Mills, with a shotgun, banging birdshot at him."

"Birdshot, Scuttle?"

"Yes, sir—a size they call Number Eight."

Lester Leith blew a meditative smoke ring at the raftered ceiling.

"Rather an unusual size of shot for a man to use in repelling a bandit, Scuttle!"

"Yes, sir, it is. But, as Mr. Mills explained to the police, one is less apt to miss with a charge of small shot. And he was most anxious, as he expressed it, to leave his marks on the bandit."

Lester Leith waved his hand in a careless gesture.

"Quite right, Scuttle. Number Eight shot will make a most uniform pattern, and it's deadly if the range is short. What happened next?"

"Well, sir, the back door of the candy store was open, because the proprietor was moving out some boxes and refuse. But the store hadn't been opened for business, so the front door was locked.

"The proprietor of the candy store ran out and locked the back door. The bandit was trapped. It took a key to open the front door and the proprietor had taken that key with him when he ran out the back door.

"The police besieged the place with tear gas and machine guns. They killed the bandit, riddled him with bullets, sir."

Lester Leith nodded. "Recovered the gems and closed the case, I take it, Scuttle?"

"No, sir. That's the funny part of it. The bandit had fifteen or twenty minutes in the candy store, and he hid the stones so cleverly that the police haven't been able to find them. They recovered the brief case, of course, and the penciled designs, and perhaps half a dozen loose stones. But there were literally dozens of the stones concealed so cleverly the police have been completely baffled.

"They identified the bandit. He was a man named Grigsby, known in the underworld as Griggy the Gat, and he had a long criminal record."

Lester Leith blew another smoke ring, extended the forefinger of his right hand, and traced the perimeter of the swirling smoke.

"I see, Scuttle. Then Griggy the Gat must have concealed the gems somewhere between Mills's shop and the dandy store, or somewhere in the candy store, when he knew that capture was inevitable?"

"Yes, sir."

"And the police can't find them, you say, Scuttle?"

"No, sir. They've looked everywhere. They've searched every inch of the candy store. They've even searched the car in which Griggy the Gat tried to make his escape from Mills's place. They simply can't find a single trace of the stones."

Lester Leith's eyes were bright now; and the valet watched him as a cat watches a mouse hole.

"Scuttle, you interest me."

"Yes, sir."

"The candy shop was wholesale or retail, Scuttle?"

"Both, sir. It's a small factory too—in the rear, sir."

"And the rubies were worth a great deal of money, Scuttle?"

"Yes, sir. Of course, the newspaper account, valuing them at a million dollars, was exaggerated. But the rajah has offered a reward of twenty thousand dollars for their return."

Leith lapsed into thought once more. Finally he flipped the cigarette into the fireplace and chuckled.

"You've thought of something, sir?"

Lester Leith regarded the valet coldly.

"One always is thinking of something, Scuttle."

The valet's face turned brick-red.

"Yes, sir. I had thought perhaps you had worked out a solution, sir."

"Scuttle, are you crazy? How could I work out a solution of where the gems are?"

The valet shrugged. "You've done it before, sir."

"Done what before, Scuttle?"

"Solved intricate crime problems just from reading what the newspapers had to say about them."

Lester Leith laughed. "Tut, tut, Scuttle, you're getting as bad as Sergeant Ackley! Many times I've thought out *possible* solutions, but no more. True, Sergeant Ackley has a theory I must be guilty of something just because I take an interest in crime clippings. He keeps hounding me with his infernal activities, suspecting me of this, suspecting me of that. And he tortures the facts to make them fit his theories. Do you know, Scuttle, an impartial observer hearing Ackley's theories might come to the conclusion I was guilty of some crime or other?"

Lester Leith watched his valet with narrowed eyes.

The valet, mindful of his duties as a valet, yet recollecting also that he was an undercover man for the police, and anxious to trap Leter Leith into some damaging admission, nodded sagely.

"Yes, sir. I've thought so myself at times."

"Thought what?"

"How convincing the sergeant's theories are, sir. You've got to admit that there's some mastermind who is doping out the solutions of baffling crimes in advance of the police. By the time the police solve the crime, this mastermind has scooped up the loot and gone. The police have only the empty satisfaction of solving the crime. They never recover the loot."

Lester Leith yawned prodigiously.

"And so Sergeant Ackley has convinced you that I'm that mastermind?"

The valet spoke cautiously, aware that he was treading on dangerous ground.

"I didn't say so, sir. I merely mentioned that sometimes Sergeant Ackley's theories sound convincing."

Lester Leith lit another cigarette.

"Tut, tut, Scuttle. You should know better. If I were this mysterious criminal the sergeant talks so much about, it stands to reason I'd have been caught long ago. You must remember the sergeant has had shadows tail me everywhere I go. He's continually popped into the apartment with his wild accusations and submitted me to search. But he's never discovered a single shred of evidence. Surely, he'd have had some proof by this time if he were at all correct."

The valet shrugged again.

"Perhaps, sir."

"Perhaps, Scuttle! You don't sound at all convinced by my line of reasoning."

"Well, sir, you must remember that it's the most difficult sort of a crime to prove—the robbing of robbers. Naturally, the one who is robbed doesn't dare to complain, since to do so would brand *him* as a criminal."

"Pshaw, Scuttle. Your reasoning is getting to be like that of the police. Besides, I think the sergeant is making a mistake."

"How so, sir?"

"In concentrating so much on the hijacker that he lets the real criminals slip away. After all, this mysterious mastermind of the sergeant's, no matter who he may be, is a public benefactor."

"A benefactor, sir?"

"Certainly, Scuttle. If we concede the man exists outside the imagination of Sergeant Ackley, we must admit that he makes it his business to detect crimes in time to strip the criminal of his ill-gotten gains. That's all society would do with the criminal if Sergeant Ackley apprehended him. The court would confiscate his loot, perhaps imprison him; but too often some slick lawyer would get him off."

"Perhaps, sir."

"No doubt about it, Scuttle!"

"No, sir, perhaps not. But you must admit that you have a mysterious trust fund which keeps growing, sir. True, that trust fund is administered for needy widows and orphans, but I understand the fund has grown so large that you have to employ a clerical staff to handle its disbursements."

Lester Leith's eye glittered.

"Indeed, Scuttle. And where did you get such detailed information about my private affairs?"

"Sergeant Ackley," blurted the valet. "He insisted on stopping me on the street and telling me his suspicions. He thinks you are just the type of man who would enjoy doping out crime solution, levying tribute from the criminal, and then turning the money into a trust fund for the unfortunate."

Lester Leith began to laugh.

"The dear sergeant! The overzealous, stupid, blundering incompetent! But we have digressed. We were talking about Mills, Griggy the Gat, and a million dollars' worth of rare gems. Do you know, Scuttle, the crime *does* interest me. How thoroughly have the police searched?"

"I understand, from the newspapers and from gossip, that they searched every nook and cranny. They probed between walls. They poked under showcases, they looked in sugar bins, they poured out barrels of syrup. They took the upholstering of the bandit's automobile to pieces."

"Did they look in the candy, Scuttle?"

"Where?"

"In the candy."

"Why—er—that is, I don't know what you mean, sir. How could one look inside of candy and how could a man hide gems in candy?"

"There were chocolate creams in this candy factory, Scuttle?"

"Yes, sir."

"It would be readily possible for a man to melt off the chocolate coating and thrust in one or two gems."

"But the candy would show it had been tampered with, sir."

"Not if it was re-dipped. By the way, Scuttle, go to this candy place and see if you can buy some of the chocolate creams that were on the upper floor of the establishment when the fighting was going on. I should like to examine them."

"Yes, sir. How many, sir?"

"Oh, quite a good supply. Say around fifty dollars' worth. And find out if there was any dipping chocolate that was warm while the bandit was cornered in the place.

"You see, Scuttle, the problem fascinates me. There are so many places in a candy store or factory where gems might be hidden. The proprietor may get his chocolate shipped to him in large thick bars. What would prevent a criminal from melting a hole in a bar of chocolate, dropping in some stones and then sealing up the chocolate with a little dipping chocolate?

"Of course, Scuttle, I'm only interested in a theoretical solution, you understand. I don't want to actually recover the gems. I only want to see if they *could* have been hidden that way.

"Now, Scuttle, I don't want any trouble about this. Telephone Sergeant Ackley and ask him if there is any possible objection to my buying candy from the store in which the bandit was killed."

The valet's mouth sagged. "Now, sir?"

"Oh, no great hurry, Scuttle. You might even drop by and ask the sergeant for his opinion. See if you can get him to scribble a note stating there's no objection on the part of the police department to my purchasing candy.

"Better run along and buy the chocolates, Scuttle—and also get me an electric soldering iron. Oh, yes, Scuttle, and you'd better get some of those hard, red cinnamon drops too."

The valet-spy oozed his huge bulk from the room, clapped a hat on his head and opened the outer door.

"Right away, sir. I shall carry out your orders to the letter, sir."

Sergeant Arthur Ackley scraped a spade-like thumbnail over the coarse stubble along the angle of his jaw. Across the table sat Edward H. Beaver, undercover man assigned to Lester Leith. The undercover man had just finished his report and Sergeant Ackley was considering it, his crafty eyes filmed with thought.

"Beaver," he said at length, "I'm going to let you in on something. We've recovered four of the rubies."

"Found them?" asked the undercover man.

Sergeant Ackley shook his head. He took a box of perfectos from the drawer of his desk and selected one, without offering the box to the man opposite.

"No, we didn't find them. We recovered them. Two were given to a girl and pawned. One was handed to a man who was mooching, and the other was dropped in the cup of a blind beggar."

Beaver's lips parted in astonishment.

"Fact. Girl named Molly Manser was standing looking at a window. She says a heavy-set man with a hat pulled low over his forehead and a patch over his left eye sidled up to her and asked her if she'd like some of the clothes on display in the window.

"She says she tried to walk away, but he grabbed her arm and pushed a couple of the rubies into her hand. She claims she broke away and ran, but the man didn't try to follow her."

Beaver twisted his lips. "Boloney," he said. "What did she do with 'em?"

"Took 'em to Gildersmith to hock."

"He knew they were hot?"

"Sure. He spotted 'em and held her until one of our men got there. Mills identified 'em instantly; says he can't be fooled on those rubies."

Beaver sighed. "Then she was one of the gang and they've managed to find out where the gems were and take 'em."

"Wait a minute," said Sergeant Ackley. "You're behind the times. We figured that, of course, and put the girl in the cooler. Half an hour later another pawnbroker telephoned in he had a ruby he wanted us to look at. We went out on the run. It was the same size, same color, same kind of cutting.

"This time a down-and-outer had brought it in. He was a panhandler, mooching the price of a drink. He picked on a heavyset guy with a hat pulled well down and a patch over the right eye. The guy told him to take the stone, hock it, and keep whatever he got out of it.

"Then, while we were questioning this guy, the telephone gave us another lead—a blind beggar who had one of the stones dropped into his cup. Naturally, he couldn't see who did it, but he heard the sound of the man's steps on the sidewalk. He said it was a heavy-set man.

"Now that sort of puts a different slant on this candy idea, eh?"

The undercover man nodded slowly.

"Maybe I'd better switch him to some other crime."

Sergeant Ackley shook his head emphatically.

"Somehow or other, those four rubies slipped through. We want to find out where and when. This guy, Leith, never has missed a bet yet. If we can use him as a hound to smell out the trail we can kill two birds with one stone.

"Besides, Mills is raising hell. He's related to one of the political big shots, and he's riding us up one side and down the other. That's just like his type. They smear publicity all over the papers that they're carrying a million dollars around with them, and then squawk when they get rolled."

Beaver teetered back and forth in the scarred chair. His brow was corrugated in thought.

"Sergeant," he suddenly whispered.

Sergeant Ackley scowled at him.

"Well?"

"Sergeant," said Beaver, "I have it. I tell you I *have* it—a scheme to frame Lester Leith! We'll get the candy, just like he said. You've got four of the rubies that were stolen. Those rubies can't be told from any of the other stolen rubies. We'll plant those rubies in the candy and hand 'em to Leith.

"After a while Leith will find those rubies. He'll salt 'em. We'll be watching him all the time and we'll nab him for possession of stolen property, for being an accessory after the fact, and"—Beaver clenched and unclenched the ham-like fist of his right hand—"for resisting an officer!"

Sergeant Ackley grinned. "Make it for resisting two officers, Beaver," and he doubled up his own right fist.

"It'll be a cinch," said Beaver. "He's got off wrong on this case and thinks the rubies are hidden in the candy. But we don't care how right or how wrong he is, just so we can get him with stolen property."

Sergeant Ackley shot his open hand across the table.

"Shake, Beaver! By George, I'll see that you get a promotion for this! It's an idea that'll stick Mr. Lester Leith inside, lookin' out."

Beaver nodded solemnly.

"All right. I'll get the candy and come back here. We'll plant the rubies. You'd better write me a note I can take to him so he'll feel I've got results. Say in the note he can buy anything he pleases so far as the department is concerned."

Sergeant Ackley squinted one eye. "It's sort of a fool letter to write."

"I know, but it will make Leith think I'm on the level with him."

Ackley nodded. "Go on out and pick up the candy. Bring it back here and we'll stick in the rubies."

It took Beaver an hour to get the candy and the soldering iron and return to headquarters. Sergeant Ackley was pacing the floor in the manner of a caged lion.

"Took you long enough, Beaver," he grunted. "Let's get busy."

"The candy in the boxes?" asked Beaver.

"Yeah. Put the rubies in the top row, one in each of four boxes. Mark the boxes and mark the candies that have the rubies in 'em. I've thought of a slick way of getting the rubies into the candy. We simply heat the rubies in a pan. Then, when they're warm, press 'em against the bottoms of the chocolates and let 'em melt in."

Beaver nodded appreciatively.

"Beats Leith's idea of the soldering iron," he agreed.

Sergeant Ackley sneered. "Leith ain't so brainy. He's just had the breaks, that's all. This idea of mine is going to put him where he belongs."

"My idea," corrected Beaver.

Sergeant Ackley scowled. "I'll let you have some of the credit, Beaver, but don't try to hog things. I thought of the idea. That is, I outlined the whole thing and was just pointing out to you how to handle it when you interrupted and took the words out of my mouth."

Beaver's jaw dropped.

They found an alcohol stove and a pan. They heated the rubies and picked up one of the chocolates. One of the hot rubies was pushed through the bottom of the chocolate.

Sergeant Ackley surveyed the result.

"Not so good. Looks kinda messy," he said.

"We can take this electric soldering iron and sort of smooth it over," said Beaver.

Ackley nodded.

"Watch out. Your fingers are melting the chocolate, leaving fingerprints on it. We don't want that. Better wear gloves. That's the way they do it in the candy factories."

They heated the iron and held it against the chocolate. When they had finished, the result was hardly artistic.

"Well," said Sergeant Ackley, "I guess it'll get by; but we won't need to mark the chocolates that have the gems in them."

"No," agreed the undercover man.

Beaver picked up the carton containing the boxes of chocolates. The last word he heard as he sidled out of Ackley's private office was a petulant comment from the sergeant.

"I'm not so sure, Beaver, that idea of yours is any good. . . ."

Lester Leith beamed on the undercover man.

"Well, well, Scuttle, you have had a busy afternoon, haven't you? And you've done nobly—the candy, the soldering iron, even a letter from Sergeant Ackley written on police stationery, stating that I can buy anything I want. That's fine!

"Now let's see if I can melt one of the candies and insert one of the red cinnamon drops. We'll pretend that the cinnamon drop represents a ruby."

Leith connected the electric soldering iron and set to work.

When he was finished, there was chocolate smeared over his fingers, his face was flushed, and three chocolate creams were now sloppy and formless.

"How long did this Griggy the Gat have in the candy shop?"

"Not more than fifteen or twenty minutes, sir."

"Then he couldn't have done it, Scuttle."

"Couldn't have done what, sir?"

"Hid the gems in the candy."

"Begging your pardon, sir. Couldn't he have done a better job if he'd heated the stones and pressed them into the chocolate, and then finished the job with the hot iron?"

Lester Leith stared at his man with narrowed eyes.

"Scuttle, have you been experimenting?"

"Not exactly, sir. That is to say—no, sir. And by the way, sir, while I think of it, I picked up a bit of gossip at headquarters. It seems four of the stones have been found by the police."

The valet told Leith how the four stones were recovered. When he had finished Lester Leith was chuckling.

"Scuttle, that's all the information I needed to give me a perfect solution to the crime."

"Yes, sir?"

"Yes, Scuttle. But of course, you understand it's only a theoretical solution, and I do not intend to put it to any practical use."

"Of course, sir."

"And now I have some errands for you before the stores close. I want you to get me four genuine pearls of the finest luster. I want a package of cornstarch. I want some quick-drying cement and some powdered alum."

The valet was rubbing his jaw.

"And, Scuttle," said Lester Leith beamingly, "you've heard of daylight saving, of course. What do you think of it?"

"It's inconvenient in the mornings, sir, but convenient in the evening."

"Yes, indeed, Scuttle. Yet a moment's thought will convince you that it hasn't saved any daylight. It's merely kidded man into believing that there is more daylight. The days aren't any longer. Man simply gets up earlier."

"Yes, sir. I guess so, sir."

"Yes, indeed, Scuttle. But it's a great plan. However, we shouldn't limit it to clock juggling. Why not carry it to its logical conclusion and have a heat-saving plan? Why not have perpetual summer?"

The valet was interested, but dazed.

"How could you do that, sir?"

"I'll show you. It's now the second of November."

"Yes, sir."

"Very well, Scuttle. You see that calendar hanging against the wall?"

"Yes, sir."

"Watch it."

And Lester Leith, stepping to the calendar, tore off the month of November. He did the same for December. Next year's calendar was underneath, and from this he removed January, February, March, April, May, and June. The month that remained on top was July.

"There we are, Scuttle. We simply set the calendar ahead eight months. We now have summer with us. See, according to the calendar it's July second. Think of what it means to suffering humanity. Summer is here, and we haven't had a single cold spell. Winter is over! Rejoice, Scuttle!"

The valet-spy sank into a chair.

"Have you gone stark raving mad?" he demanded.

"No," said Lester Leith, pursing his lips judiciously. "I think not, Scuttle. Why do you suggest it?"

"But, good Lord, sir, simply tearing off the calendar won't make summer come any quicker."

"Why, you surprise me, Scuttle. You admit daylight saving gives us an hour more of daylight."

"Well, that's different. You said yourself it was merely a scheme by which men kid themselves."

"Certainly, Scuttle. And that's all tearing off the leaves of the calendar does. Come, come, Scuttle, enter into the spirit of the thing. It's the second of July and you've got the heat on. Shut the heat off, and then start out and get me the pearls and the cornstarch and the alum, and quick-drying cement. And you had better get a small crucible and a blowtorch too.

"Some of the things you'll have to pay cash for, Scuttle. The pearls you can charge. Get them at Hendricksen's, and he can telephone me for an okay on the order if he wishes. But get started, Scuttle. Even in these long summer days the stores close promptly at five o'clock."

"It isn't summer, sir, it's the second day of November."

"Tut, tut, Scuttle, don't be such an old fossil! Adapt yourself to the times!"

The valet, shaking his head, shut off the steam heat and slipped from the apartment. Lester Leith opened the windows, and the cold of the late November afternoon crept into the room.

From a public telephone booth Scuttle reported to

Sergeant Ackley and his report sounded strangely garbled.

Sergeant Ackley muttered a curse over the wire.

"Beaver, you've been drinking."

"No, sir, I haven't. I swear I haven't had a drop. Go on out there and see for yourself, if you don't believe me. I tell you he's gone crazy. He had me shutting off the heat just before I left. And he insists that it's July according to this crazy calendar saving time of his. Go there, if you don't believe it."

"By George, I *will* go out there!" yelled Sergeant Ackley.

Which was why, as Lester Leith sat bundled to the ears in a fur coat, there was an imperative rap on the door.

He arose and opened it.

Sergeant Ackley glared at him.

"H'lo, Leith. Happened to be in the neighborhood and dropped in to see you."

Lester Leith gathered the fur coat about him.

"Is this an official visit, Sergeant?"

"Well, not exactly."

"You haven't a warrant either for search or arrest?"

"Good Lord, no! I tell you I just dropped in."

"Very well, then, it's a social visit. Do come in, Sergeant, and sit down. It's a little chilly for July. In fact, I don't remember when there's been a cooler summer."

The sergeant stared at Lester Leith.

"A cooler summer! Dammit, man, it's winter."

Lester Leith positively beamed.

"By George, that's so. I forgot to tell you of my new heat-saving scheme. It's the same as daylight saving. That is, it depends on the same psychological factors, and it's equally logical.

"You see, like every great idea, it's simple. We achieve daylight saving simply by setting our clocks ahead. Well, I've achieved heat saving by the same method. I've set the calendar ahead. I tear off eight months and make it July. It's marvelously simple!"

Sergeant Ackley peered intently at Lester Leith.

"You're cuckoo," he said. "It's freezing in here. You'll catch your death of cold. Good Lord, sitting in a room with the windows all up and thermometer down to freezing!"

Sergeant Ackley sat on the edge of a chair and shivered.

"Hello, what's the idea of all the candy?" he asked.

"Just a whim, Sergeant. I was thinking about that unfortunate robbery of Mr. Mills, and I wondered if it was possible that the criminal had concealed the rubies in some of the candy."

"So you sent out and bought this candy. Did it ever occur to you that you'd have been in rather a bad position if the candy *had* contained the gems?"

Lester Leith smiled frankly.

"Of course, Sergeant. That's why I had my man call on you and get permission in writing to purchase anything he wanted."

Sergeant Ackley's brows knitted.

"But it was all a mistake. The hiding couldn't have been worked that way. Have a piece of candy, Sergeant."

Lester Leith extended a box and the sergeant took a chocolate, taking care to inspect the bottom before he sank his teeth into it.

For several seconds he toyed with the candy, going through the motions of eating it, yet making little headway. All of a sudden he stiffened and looked at the candy between his forefinger and thumb. Then he looked at the insides of the thumb and forefinger, and sat upright in his chair.

"Something?" asked Lester Leith politely.

But Sergeant Ackley was halfway to the door.

"You devil!" he exclaimed. "You clever devil!"

And the door banged behind him.

Lester Leith gazed at the door with a puzzled frown.

Sergeant Ackley sprinted for the elevator and literally ran into Beaver at the sidewalk. He shot out a huge hand and scooped Beaver into an alcove.

"He ain't crazy," said Sergeant Ackley. "I don't know what his game is, but it's the cleverest scheme ever pulled in a criminal case."

Beaver, his arms filled with packages, surveyed his superior with blinking eyes.

"Have *you* gone daffy too?"

Sergeant Ackley shook his head.

"Look here," he said, "when we heated the gems and tried to put them in the chocolate creams, what happened?"

"Why, we messed the job up," admitted Beaver.

"Right," said Sergeant Ackley. "Chocolate melts at about the heat of human blood, see? Well, if you hadn't been such a damned fool you'd have remembered the room was steam-heated. That's what made the chocolates messy! Now Lester Leith is sitting up there with the heat off and the windows open. The room is freezing. But look what it did to the chocolates! You can hold one of them in your fingers for minutes and it won't get sloppy. You could slip a hot stone into those chocolates and cover up the place by holding a hot iron near the chocolate, and make a perfect job of it. And you could do it quick!"

The valet-spy's jaw sagged.

"Of course! And the loft of the candy store was cold when Griggy the Gat was in there!"

Sergeant Ackley nodded.

"I'm glad to see that you're not entirely hopeless, Beaver. Now you get up to that apartment and humor Lester Leith in this heat-saving idea of his. Give him all the rope he wants. Put on an overcoat and let the room get just as cold as he wants it. And be sure to keep your eye on that candy!"

"How about the candy that's still out at the candy factory?"

Sergeant Ackley chuckled.

"That's where I'm going right now. I'm going to have the police buy up every ounce of that candy, all the chocolate and all the mixing cream, and I'm going to put them all in one great big pot and melt them down. Then I'm going to pour off the syrup and see what's left. I have an idea we'll have the rest of those gems!"

"Meaning," asked Beaver, "that there are stones in the candy upstairs?"

Sergeant Ackley nodded.

"And we spent the afternoon putting more stones in it!"

"That," snapped Sergeant Ackley, "was *your* idea, Beaver. Now go up there and watch him like a hawk. When we get ready to spring the trap we'll spring it right."

When Beaver entered the apartment, Lester Leith was wrapped in a fur overcoat, his ankles covered with a wool blanket.

"Ah, good evening, Scuttle. Back already. Do you know, Scuttle, I can't remember ever having seen a colder summer!"

The valet peered at the calendar.

"Here it is July already, and cold. Sometimes June is rather cool, but it's unusual July weather, sir."

Lester Leith smiled and nodded.

"Very well spoken. You got the things for me?"

The valet nodded.

Lester Leith idly reached for a chocolate cream. The valet watched him intently.

Lester Leith's hand went to his mouth. He pushed some red object into the palm of his hand with his tongue, and his face lit with a smile of satisfaction.

The valet knew it was not one of the pieces he and Sergeant Ackley had loaded with the four rubies, so he leaned forward eagerly.

"Something, sir?" he asked, his voice trembling.

Lester Leith dropped the red object into his pocket.

"Yes, Scuttle, one of the red cinnamon drops. I forgot that I had put them in the chocolates, and cinnamon drops don't mix very well with cream."

There was a knock on the door. The valet eased his bulk toward the door and opened it. A dark-haired young woman with a very red mouth stood on the threshold. Her eyes were sparkling from the crisp air of the winter night.

"Which one of you is Lester Leith?" she asked.

Leith got to his feet as the girl walked into the cold room and the valet closed the door.

"Heat off?" asked the girl.

Lester Leith held a chair for her.

"Yes," he said. "I am trying an experiment in heat saving."

"Well, you're saving it all right. . . . . All right, what are you giving away?"

Leith explained to his valet. "I telephoned a friend of mine and told him I had a gift for a deserving young lady." Then turning to their visitor, "I want to give you some candy. I made a rather large candy purchase on a speculation which didn't turn out, and I'm left with the candy on my hands."

The valet-spy said, "You wouldn't give it away, sir—"

Lester Leith said coldly, "That will do, Scuttle." He turned again to the girl. "If you think your—er—boy friend would misinterpret the spirit which prompts this gift, I should be glad to deliver it to you in his presence."

The girl's eyes narrowed.

Leith continued, "I'll carry the candy down to a cab."

She was sizing him up with eyes accustomed to making fast and accurate appraisals. In the end she reached the verdict which most women reached with Lester Leith.

"Okay," she said.

Leith loaded his arms with candy boxes and escorted the woman to the door.

"I'll help you carry some of the boxes down, sir," said Scuttle.

Lester Leith shook his head. "You stay right here, Scuttle."

And he led the way to the elevator, made two more trips back for candy, and then wished the police spy a good night.

"You'll be back soon, sir?" asked the valet, noticing that Lester Leith had evening clothes under his overcoat.

Lester Leith smiled. "Scuttle," he said, "I am an opportunist."

And the outer door clicked as the spring lock shot into place.

The spy made a lunge for the telephone, where he called Sergeant Ackley and poured out a report which made the sergeant mutter exclamations of anger.

"Dammit, Beaver, he couldn't have given away *all* the candy!"

"But he did."

"And he went with her?"

"Yes."

"Well, I've got shadows on the job. They'll tail him."

"Yes, Sergeant, I know, but how about the candy? The

shadows will tail Leith, but they won't tail the girl after Leith leaves her. She'll have the candy, and the candy's got a bunch of rubies and diamonds in it—"

"Damn that fool idea of *yours*, Beaver. Get down and tell those shadows to forget Leith and tail the candy. Tail that *candy*."

But by the time Beaver reached the sidewalk there was no trace of Leith, the girl, or the candy. Nor, of course, of the shadows. Following instructions, they had tailed Lester Leith.

It was well past midnight when Lester Leith returned. He scowled at his valet.

"Tut, tut, Scuttle, you have turned the heat on! Here I work out a new calendar arrangement that's to be a boon to mankind, and you spoil it all. It's July, Scuttle! One doesn't have steam heat on in July!"

The valet could only raise his tired eyes.

Leith softened. "Scuttle, I'll have some errands for you to do in the morning."

"Yes, sir."

"Ring up Sergeant Ackley and tell him I have a valuable clue on the Mills robbery. Then I want you to remember our patriotic obligations."

"Patriotic obligations, sir?"

"Quite right, Scuttle. Notice the date."

"It's the second—no, it's the third of November."

"No, no, it's the third of July! And on the fourth we celebrate the anniversary of the independence of our country. I shall want some firecrackers, Scuttle, and some slow-match—'punk,' I think it's called. You can get them all at one of the Chinese stores. They keep firecrackers, not as seasonal merchandise, but as a staple."

"Lord, sir, are you really going to celebrate the fourth of July on the fourth of November?"

"Certainly, Scuttle. I presume you are not attempting to criticize me?"

"No, sir. I shall attend to the matter in the morning, sir."

"That's fine, Scuttle, and I wish you'd get me a siren."

"A what?"

"One of the electric sirens such as are used on police cars, Scuttle."

"But it's against the law to have one on your car unless you're an officer, sir."

"I didn't say anything about putting it on my car. I merely said I wanted one."

The valet nodded, then left, his expression more puzzled than ever.

For more than an hour Leith sat and smoked. From time to time he nodded his head as if he were checking the moves in a complicated game.

At the end of an hour he chuckled.

The morning was still young when Lester Leith was aroused by his valet.

"I'm sorry, sir, but it's Sergeant Ackley. You remember you told me to tell him you had a clue on the Mills robbery? Well, sir, Sergeant Ackley wouldn't wait. He's in the apartment now."

Leith stretched and yawned.

"Quite right, Scuttle. The sergeant is only doing his duty. Show him in."

The valet opened the door and Sergeant Ackley strode into the room.

"Well," said the sergeant. "What's the dope on Mills?"

Leith sat up.

"You doubtless know, Sergeant, that I sent my valet for some candy to the same firm where Griggy the Gat was killed after the robbery. I had a theory that the thief might have put some of the stones in the candy, and—"

Sergeant Ackley rubbed his tired, red-rimmed eyes.

"Well, you can forget that! Thanks to that idea of yours, I had my men put in most of the night melting down every bit of candy and chocolate in the place. And we got nothing—absolutely nothing!"

"Did you now?" said Lester Leith. "That's strange, because I gave away my candy last night to a very beautiful young lady. When I left her she insisted that I eat some candy, and would you believe it, Sergeant, when I bit into that piece of candy there were three foreign substances in the filling!"

Sergeant Ackley's cigar dropped.

"Three!" he yelled.

"Yes, Sergeant, three. One of them was a cinnamon drop I'd put in myself earlier in the evening when I was experimenting, and the other were two red stones. I feel quite certain they are rubies. And I'm wondering, Sergeant, if perhaps they aren't some of the stolen loot."

Lester Leith reached in the pocket of his pajamas and took out a handkerchief. In this handkerchief was a knot, which, on being loosened, revealed two large rubies of such deep fire and so perfectly matched that they looked like two drops of jeweled pigeon-blood.

"Both in the *same* piece of candy?" asked Sergeant Ackley.

"Both in the same piece, Sergeant."

Sergeant Ackley framed his next question with a carelessness that was far too elaborate.

"Don't know where the girl is? The one that you gave the candy to?"

Lester Leith shook his head.

The sergeant turned to the door.

"Going to see her again?"

Lester Leith shrugged. Then he said brightly, "You want to help me celebrate the fourth, Sergeant?"

"The fourth?"

"Of July, you know."

"Why, dammit, this is November."

"Oh, no, Sergeant, this is July. My new calendar calls—"

"Oh, hell!" stormed the sergeant, and slammed the door behind him.

Outdoors, he called the police shadows and gave them instructions.

"Tail Leith until he brings you to the candy or to the girl that's got the candy. After that, drop Leith and tail the candy. Get me? I want that candy!"

The police shadows saluted and returned to their stations. They waited for more than an hour before Lester Leith emerged.

Nor was it any secret to Lester Leith that the police shadows were waiting for him. He walked up to them.

"Gentlemen, good morning. So you won't have any trouble following me, I am going to get a taxicab. I will go directly to the Mills shop, where I will talk with Mr. Mills, the gentleman who was robbed. If you should lose me at any stage of the journey you can go directly there."

In the Mills shop Lester Leith became all business.

"Mr. Mills, what would you say to a process which produced wonderful pearls at a small cost? The best experts would swear they were genuine."

Mr. Carter Mills was a heavyset man with an undershot jaw and a leering eye.

"Nonsense," he said. "You're just another fool with another synthetic pearl scheme. Get out!"

Lester Leith took a pearl from his pocket and rolled it across the desk.

"Keep that as a souvenir of my visit," he said.

The jeweler picked up the pearl between his thumb and forefinger and was about to throw it away when he caught sight of the smooth sheen. He opened a drawer, took out a magnifying glass, and focused it on the pearl. Then he pressed a button on the side of his desk.

Lester Leith lit a cigarette.

The door of the private office opened and a man entered.

"Markle," snapped Mills, "take a look at this and tell me what it is."

The man nodded to Lester Leith, took a glass from his pocket, accepted the pearl from Mills, and studied it attentively. After nearly a minute Markle pronounced his verdict.

"It's a genuine pearl. Luster is good and it has a good shape."

Mills took the pearl from the man's cupped hand and jerked an authoritative thumb toward the door. Markle nodded once more to Leith and glided through the door.

Mills's eyes turned to Leith.

"You try to run a bunco on me and I'll have you jugged!"

Lester Leith took from his pocket a little globule of dead-looking white substance. It was, in fact, a combination of cornstarch and alum, dissolved in quick-drying waterproof cement.

"What's that?" asked the jeweler.

"Another pearl—or it will be when I've subjected it to my special process."

Mills examined it under the magnifying glass.

"Huh," he said. "There isn't any money in selling synthetic pearls."

"What's more, I haven't any money to put into equipment," said Leith.

The jeweler grinned. "All right. Let's have it."

"You will announce," said Lester Leith, "that you have found a wonderful pearl deposit off the Mexican coast. That deposit will be there, and your divers will actually bring up the pearls. But I will have first planted those pearls where the divers will find them. We will market the pearls at ridiculously low prices, and then, at the proper moment, sell the pearl bed."

Mills blinked his eyes.

"You mean to salt a pearl mine?"

"And rake in a few million profit from doing it."

Mills looked shrewdly at Leith.

"It's illegal," he said. "If we were caught we would be jailed for fraud."

"If we were caught," admitted Leith.

The jeweler clasped his hands across his stomach.

"How would you keep from getting caught?"

"I," said Lester Leith, "would keep you completely in the background. You would simply give me sufficient money to salt the field. I would plant pearls in the oysters. Then I would communicate with you and you would discover the field. You would be perfectly safe."

"What made you come to me?"

"I read of your loss of the rajah's gems in the paper. I knew the publicity would result unfavorably for you and that your legitimate business would suffer for a while. It occurred to me you might be interested."

Mills squinted his eyes.

"Yet, after what you've told me, you don't dare to go to anyone else."

"Why?"

"I'd know too much. I could expose the deal."

Lester Leith smiled. "That's supposing you turn it down. You're not such a fool as to pass up millions of dollars in order to keep me from putting across a deal with someone else."

Mills sighed. "I'll look into the process and see how it works."

Lester Leith nodded.

"I'll meet you anywhere you want tomorrow morning and give you a complete demonstration."

Mills got to his feet.

"Tomorrow morning at nine o'clock at my house. I don't do important business here. There are too many eyes and ears. My house is my castle. Here's the address."

Lester Leith took the card.

"Tomorrow at nine."

Lester Leith loaded his car with a miscellaneous assortment of things which seemed to have no connection with each other.

There was a suitcase containing the blowtorch and the crucible. There was a package of cornstarch, of powdered alum, of waterproof, quick-drying cement. There was another suitcase containing firecrackers.

There was a siren, a battery, and an electrical connection. There were pliers and wires. There was, in fact, such a weird assortment as to make it seem that Lester Leith was going into the junk business.

But the police knew the unusual methods by which Lester Leith had managed in the past to solve crimes and hijack the criminals, and they watched Leith with cautious eyes.

And always the shadows were mindful of their instructions—whenever Leith should meet the girl, the shadows were to drop Leith and tail the candy.

If Leith knew of their instructions he gave no sign. He drove the car down the boulevard, trailed by a police car.

The shadows were the best in the business. Yet the sedan which slipped between them and Lester Leith had been there for several blocks before the police realized that the two people in the sedan were also tailing Lester Leith.

The police dropped back.

The three cars threaded their way through the crowded streets and came at length to a more open stretch of the countryside. Leith's car gathered speed. The sedan rushed close behind it, and the police were forced to push the needle high up on their speedometer to keep their quarry in sight.

Lester Leith slowed his car at a place where there was a vacant stretch of field, a bordering strip of woods, and a stone wall.

The sedan also slid to a stop.

The roadside was deserted. For the police to have stopped in that particular place would have meant they must disclose their identity, so they slipped past the parked cars. But they slowed their speed enough so that the two men who occupied the police car could see just who it was Leith was talking with. And what they saw brought smiles to their faces. For Lester Leith was talking with the girl who had called at his apartment, and the man with her was undoubtedly her boy friend. But, what was more to the point, they glimpsed boxes of candy in the rear of the sedan.

The detectives piloted their car around a curve in the road, then slipped into the shelter of a stone wall. A pair of powerful binoculars gave them a good view of what was taking place.

Lester Leith seemed very well acquainted. The man was not quite as smiling as the girl, but the girl was effusively cordial. After an interval of conversation a flask was produced, also a picnic lunch. The trio ate lunch while the detectives made notes of exactly what was happening.

Following lunch, the detectives received a surprise. Their instructions had been to shadow Leith to the candy, and after that, to follow the candy until it was possible to communicate with Sergeant Ackley. But Ackley had advised them that it was a million-to-one shot that Leith would never separate himself from that candy.

Yet Leith climbed into his car and drove down the road, directly toward the detectives. The girl and her escort got into their sedan and drove back toward town.

There was no doubt as to the detectives' instructions.

They took after the sedan.

The sedan hit the through boulevard some ten miles from town and started along it, traveling at a steady rate of speed.

"Looks like they're going right in, Louis," said the officer at the wheel. "I better drop you at the corner. Telephone headquarters, then stop a car and catch up with me."

The police car came to a stop before a drug store, the shadow jumped to the ground, and was gone.

He notified Sergeant Ackley of the separation of Leith and the candy.

The sergeant got the location of the cars, their probable course, and ordered the shadow to get back to his companion as quickly as possible.

Within six miles, after commandeering a passing car, the detective rejoined his partner.

The cars continued their journey. The first important cross street brought them to a stop. Another police car slipped from the curb and the two shadows identified the sedan ahead by making signs.

What followed was short and snappy. The second police car forged ahead and abreast of the sedan. There was the sound of a siren, the motioning of uniformed arms, and the sedan slid to the curb. The driver leaned out to shout comments.

"Can't help it," said the officer in charge. "You folks have been driving recklessly. You'll have to come to headquarters and explain it to the sergeant. Bill, get over there in the sedan and see that they follow."

One of the officers pushed the candy boxes to one side and sat down on the rear seat.

At headquarters in the private office of Sergeant Ackley, the sergeant gazed shrewdly at the captive before turning his eyes to the candy.

"Come through and come clean," he said.

"What," asked the man, "is the real charge?"

"Robbery."

"What?"

"You've got close to a million dollars' worth of stolen gems concealed in that candy."

There could be no mistaking their genuine astonishment.

"You got those boxes from a chap named Leith," said Ackley, "and the candy in them is loaded with the rubies and diamonds stolen from Mills."

The sergeant opened a box, bit into a piece of chocolate, chewed it up, and muttered his surprise as he found nothing except chocolate and cream filling. He bit into another, and the frown left his face. He twisted his tongue around, held his cupped hand before his mouth, and pushed a red object into the palm.

"Here's one of 'em," he said.

They crowded around him. Ackley lowered his palm. It contained a red cinnamon drop, stained with melted chocolate.

In the silence which followed, the girl's titter sounded like an explosion. The man nudged her, Ackley reached for another piece of candy.

Once more the sergeant drew a red cinnamon drop.

"He switched before he gave you the candy!" he said.

The girl was fingering the chocolates. "I don't think so. This top row seems to have been handled, but the other row doesn't, and it's just in this box. Wait a minute. Here's one—"

Ackley grabbed it, broke it open. He pulled out a small object from the interior, then let out a yell.

"This is one!"

It was a blood-red ruby. Then Ackley cursed again.

"Hell, this is the one I planted there myself!"

And he started breaking open the chocolate creams.

His hands became soggy messes, but he found no more rubies.

"Where's Leith?" he asked.

He might as well have asked the wind what had become of the breeze. For Lester Leith, taking advantage of the absence of shadows, had disappeared.

His apartment remained untenanted, save for the undercover man. His garage remained empty. Lester Leith was somewhere in the teeming city, lying low, waiting for his appointment with Mr. Carter Mills.

And Sergeant Ackley sat back in his swivel chair,

blamed his subordinates, and continued to curse.

The entire staff at headquarters was munching chocolate creams and waiting.

Lester Leith, in the living room of Mills's suburban house, set up a blowtorch, a crucible, took a package of cornstarch and some powdered alum from his suitcase. Then he took some waterproof cement, and sat cross-legged on the floor.

"Unfortunate robbery you had the other day," he said as he poured a small quantity of cornstarch into the crucible.

Mills grunted.

Leith took a vial from his pocket and handed it to Mills. His greedy eyes devoured the luster of the pearls in the vial.

"We can make our fortune out of this," Mills said and glanced back to the crucible.

To his surprise he found himself looking into the business end of an automatic which had appeared in Leith's hand while Mills's attention had been on the pearls.

Leith smiled. "Take it easy, Mills. You're dealing with big stuff now."

"What do you mean?"

"I'm a gangster. I use gangsters' methods. I've got a mob that'll stop at nothing. Griggy the Gat was one of my men."

Beads of perspiration stood out on the jeweler's forehead. He kept his eyes on the gun.

"You see, you made up your mind a long time ago to steal those gems from the rajah," went on Lester Leith, his voice ominously smooth. "So you deliberately arranged for a lot of newspaper publicity about how you carried a million dollars in gems back and forth from your work.

"Naturally I fell for it. I told Griggy the Gat to get into your place, collar you when you came in, and grab the stones. Griggy muffed the job, but mostly because you had it all figured out. You knew a clever yeggman would probably strike just when you entered your place of business in the morning.

"You're smart, Mills, and that's why you always came to work a few minutes before anyone else showed up. You gave a stickup just that opening, hoping he'd fall.

"What happened was just what you hoped for—that the stickup would get killed in a gun battle with the cops.

"Griggy the Gat got the bum breaks, you got the good ones. The bulls looked all over and couldn't find the stones. That was natural—because they hadn't been in the brief case in the first place!

"Then you made a fool move. You were afraid the police would reach the right conclusion when they searched every place they could think of and still didn't find the stones. You wanted to convince them that the gems *had* been stolen. So you started to put some of them in circulation.

"You were clever enough to know that the average person never remembers more than one distinctive feature, or two at the most. You pulled a cap well down on your head and put a patch over one eye. Those two things were obvious. The people you dealt with saw them, and saw nothing else. But you made a mistake when you had the patch over the left eye on one occasion, and over the right on another. Yet you fooled the police."

"What do you want?" asked Mills.

"A cut, of course."

Mills wet his lips. "You can't prove a thing. I'm not going to be held up."

Lester Leith glanced at his watch.

"It may interest you to know," he said, "that the police have at last reached the conclusion they should have reached before. Having decided that the gems were not concealed by Griggy the Gat, and having convinced themselves the gems weren't on Griggy at the time of his death, they have concluded you didn't give them to Griggy. Therefore, they have decided you slipped over a fast one. So they took your picture, made a life-size enlargement, put a cap on it and a patch over one eye, and the witnesses have identified it as the man who gave out four of the rubies."

Mills swallowed with difficulty.

Lester Leith holstered his gun.

"After all, it's not my funeral. I've decided to have the gang take you for a little vacation. At a signal from me they'll come in. If you don't kick through with the gems you'll go for a ride."

Mills squirmed.

"You said the police—"

Leith glanced at his watch again.

"Are on their way. Guess I'd better call in the boys."

Mills choked.

"Last chance," smiled Leith.

Mills shook his head.

"No. You're wrong. I haven't got them. I—"

He broke off. From the east sounded the wail of a siren, a wail that grew in volume.

"Save me, the police!" screamed Mills.

Leith struck him across the face.

"Save you, you cheap crook—save myself! Save my boys. They're out there covering me. If the police stop here it'll mean a massacre!"

Mills dived toward a window.

Leith's fist crashed into his jaw and sent him down to the floor.

"You damn fool. Keep away from that window. The police will walk right into an ambush. My choppers will mow them down. You know what that means. When you kill a cop there's always hell to pay."

The siren keened even louder.

"Seems to be right in my garage!" said Mills.

"Then listen for firing," said Leith.

Bang! Bang! Bang! Poppety-pop-pop-pop Bang!

"Riot guns!" yelled Leith.

For a space of seconds the explosions continued, and then silence descended.

Leith sighed. "Well, you've done it. My men have wiped out the cops—it's a massacre. Naturally, the bulls will blame you for the job. It's the chair for you—unless—"

"Unless what?"

"Unless I decide to take you into the gang. We can use a good jewel man."

Mills struggled to his hands and knees.

"I won't stand for it. I'll stay right here and explain to the officers."

Leith laughed grimly.

"Listen, fat guy," he said. "My men have just mowed down a squad of bluecoats. Think I'm going to get soft over one more murder?"

He took out his automatic, sighted it. His eyes gleamed with the fury popularly supposed to possess a murderer at the moment of the kill.

"No, no! I'll kick through, wait!"

Mills scrambled to his feet, scuttled to the hall, and took a thick cane from the hall tree where it had been hanging in plain sight.

"Here they are," he said, thrusting the cane into Leith's hands. "Come on, quick. I'll throw in with you!"

Lester Leith shook the cane.

"No, no. You can't tell by shaking. It's balanced with sheet lead and stuffed with cotton. The gems are nested in the cotton. You get into it by unscrewing the ferrule."

"All right, Mills," Leith said. "Better go out to your garage and start sweeping up the firecrackers. And you'll find a siren connected so that it would start to wail when a piece of punk burned through a connection, just before the firecrackers went off. I was celebrating the fourth of July."

Mills tried to speak, but the sounds that came out were not words.

"Good morning," said Lester Leith.

"The—the—police!" stuttered Mills.

"Oh, yes, the police. They are still groping in the dark. I solved the case because the police proved my suspicions by a process of elimination. You see, your inordinate desire for newspaper publicity made me a little suspicious at the first. Then when the police looked everywhere that Griggy might have concealed the stones and didn't find a trace, my suspicion became a certainty."

And Lester Leith strolled from the front door with all the ease of a man who is very sure of himself.

Sergeant Ackley was pacing the floor of Leith's apartment when Lester Leith entered.

"Well, well, Sergeant! Waiting for me?"

Sergeant Ackley spoke with the slow articulation of a man who is trying to control his rage.

"Get the stones?" he asked.

Lester Leith raised his eyebrows.

"Pardon?"

Sergeant Ackley took a deep breath.

"You ditched the shadows yesterday and disappeared!"

Lester Leith lit a cigarette.

"Sit down, Sergeant. You're frightfully fidgety. Overwork, I guess. No, Sergeant, as it happened your shadows ditched me."

"Well," growled the officer, "either way, you disappeared and didn't come home last night."

Leith's smile became a chuckle.

"Purely a private affair, Sergeant."

"Then you called on Mills and set off a bunch of firecrackers."

"Quite right, Sergeant. This is the fourth of July, you know, according to my special heat-saving calendar. I was celebrating. Mills didn't complain, did he?"

Sergeant Ackley twisted the cigar from the left side of his mouth to the right.

"That," he said, "is the funny part of the whole thing. Mills seems to think there isn't any cause for making a squawk. And I ain't satisfied about that candy yet. There are some things in this caper I've missed. That girl and her boy friend, for instance—couldn't even hold them, no evidence. Couldn't be they were working for you, Leith, in your pay?"

Lester Leith smiled. "Tut, tut, Sergeant, you *couldn't* have missed anything."

Sergeant Ackley headed for the door.

"Leith, I think you're a crook. Sort of a supercrook, a lucky crook—but a crook. Someday I'm going to get you."

Ackley paused on the threshold.

"Next time the instructions will be what they should have been this time, and every time—*tail Leith!*"

And the door slammed.

Lester Leith turned beamingly to his valet, who had been standing by during the interview.

"Scuttle, I feel that a heat-saving calendar isn't as simple as it seemed. Turn on the heat full force, and then see if you can't pick up a new calendar somewhere. I'm going back to November."

"Now that the firecrackers are exploded," said the valet.

Lester Leith smiled again.

"Certainly, Scuttle. You wouldn't expect me to carry over a big investment in firecrackers, would you?"

The valet sighed resignedly.

"Begging your pardon, sir, I'd expect you to do almost anything—and get away with it, sir."

TO STRIKE A MATCH
(The House of Three Candles)

The Love of Loyalty Road in Canton is a wide thoroughfare cut ruthlessly through the congested district in order to modernize the city. Occasional side streets feed the traffic of automobiles and rickshaws into it, but back of these streets one enters the truly congested areas, where people live like sardines in a tin.

The Street of the Wild Chicken is so wide that one may travel down it in a ricksha. But within a hundred feet of the intersection of The Street of the Wild Chicken and The Love of Loyalty Road, one comes to *Tien Mah Hong*, which, being translated, means The Alley of the Sky Horse. And in *Tien Mah Hong* there is no room for even ricksha traffic. Two pedestrians wearing wide-brimmed hats must tilt their heads as they meet, so that the brims will not scrape as the wearers pass each other shoulder to shoulder.

Houses on each side of *Tien Mah Hong*, with balconies and windows abutting directly on The Alley of the Sky Horse, give but little opportunity for privacy. The lives of neighbors are laid bare with an intimacy of detail which would be inconceivable in a less congested community or a more occidental atmosphere. At night the peddlers of bean cakes, walking through The Alley of the Sky Horse, beat little drums to attract attention, and shout their wares with a cry which is like the howl of a wolf.

Leung Fah walked down The Alley of the Sky Horse with downcast eyes, as befitted a modest woman of the coolie class. Her face was utterly without expression. Not even the shrewdest student of human nature could have told from her outward appearance the thoughts which were seething within her breast.

It had been less than a month before that Leung Fah had clasped to her breast a morsel of humanity which represented all life's happiness, a warm, ragged bundle, a child without a father, a secret outlet for her mother love.

Then one night there had been a scream of sirens, a panic-stricken helterskelter rush of shouting inhabitants, and, over all, the ominous, steady roar of airplane engines, a hideous undertone of sound which mounted until it became as the hum of a million metallic bees.

It is easy enough to advocate fleeing to a place of safety, but the narrow roads of Canton admit of no swift handling of crowds. And there are no places of safety. Moreover, the temperament of the Chinese makes it difficult to carry out any semblance of an air-defense program. Death in one form or another is always jeering at their elbows. Why dignify one particular form of death by going to such great lengths so far as precautions are concerned?

The devil's eggs began to fall from the sky in a screaming hail. Anti-aircraft guns roared a reply. Machine guns sputtered away hysterically. Through all the turmoil the enemy flyers went calmly about their business of murder, ignoring the frenzied, nervous attempts of an unprepared city to make some semblance of defense.

With fierce mother instinct Leung Fah had held her baby to her breast, shielding it with her frail body, as though interposing a layer of flesh and bone would be of any avail against the "civilized" warfare which rained down from the skies.

The earth had rocked with a series of detonations, and then suddenly Leung Fah had been surrounded by a terrific noise, by splintered timbers, dust and debris.

When she had wiped her eyes and looked at the little morsel of humanity in her arms, she had screamed in terrified anguish.

No one had known of Leung Fah's girl. Because she had no husband, she had kept her offspring as a secret; and because she slept in one of the poorest sections of the city, where people are as numerous and as transient as bats in a cave, she had been able to maintain her secret.

Since no one had known of her child, no one had known of her loss. Night after night she had gone about her work, morsel of humanity in her arms, she had screamed in terher face an expressionless mask.

Sahm Seuh, the man who had only three fingers on his right hand, and whose eyes were cunning, moving as smoothly moist in their sockets as the tongue of a snake, had noticed her going about her work, and of late he had become exceedingly solicitous. She was not looking well. Was she perhaps sick? She no longer laughed, or paused to gossip in loud tones with the slave girls in the early morning hours before daylight. Was it perhaps that the money she was making was not sufficient? . . . Sahm Seuh's oily eyes slithered expressively. Perhaps that too could be remedied.

Because she had said nothing, because she had stared at him with eyes that saw not and ears that heard not, her soul numbed by an anguish which made her as one who walks in sleep at the hour of the rat, Sahm Seuh grew bold.

Did she need money? Lots of money—gold money? Not the paper money of China, but gold which would enable her to be independent? *Aiii-ahh*. It was simple. As simple as the striking of a match. And Sahm Seuh flipped his wrist in a quick motion and scratched a match into flame to illustrate his meaning. He went away then, leaving her to think the matter over.

That night, as she moved through the narrow thoroughfares of the city, her mind brooded on the words of Seuh. . . .

Canton is a sleepless city of noise. At times, during the

summer months, there comes a slight ebb of activity during the first few hours after midnight, but it is an ebb which is barely perceptible to occidental ears. In the large Chinese cities people sleep in shifts because there is not enough room to accommodate them all at one time in houses. Those who are off-shift roam the streets, and because Chinese ears are impervious to noise, just as Chinese nostrils are immune to smells, the hubbub of conversation continues unabated.

Daylight was dawning, a murky, humid dawn which brought renewed heat to a city already steeped in its own emanations—a city of silent-winged mosquitoes, oppressive and sweltering heat, unevaporated perspiration, and those odors which cling to China as an aura.

Sahm Seuh stood suddenly before her.

"That gold?" he asked. "Do you wish it?"

"I would strike a match," she said tonelessly.

"Meet me," Sahm Seuh said, "at the house in The Alley of the Sky Horse where three candles burn. Open the door and climb the stairs. The time is tonight, at the last minute of the hour of the dog."

And so, as one in a daze, Leung Fah turned down The Alley of the Sky Horse and shuffled along with leaden feet, her eyes utterly without expression, set in a face of wood. . . .

Night found her turning into The Alley of the Sky Horse.

In a house on the left a girl was playing a metallic-sounding Chinese harp. Ten steps back of her a bean peddler raised his voice in a long, howling "o-w-w-w-w-e-o-o-o-o." Fifty feet ahead, a family sought to scatter evil spirits by flinging lighted firecrackers from the balcony.

Leung Fah plodded on, circling a bonfire where paper imitation money, a model sedan chair, and slaves in effigy were being sent by means of fire to join the spirits of ancestors. Three candles flickered on the sidewalk in the heavy air of the hot night.

Leung Fah opened the door and climbed stairs. There was darkness ahead, only darkness. She entered a room and sensed that others were present. She could hear their breathing, the restless motions of their bodies, the rustle of clothes, occasionally a nervous cough. The hour struck—the passing of the hour of the dog, and the beginning of the hour of the boar.

The voice of Sahm Seuh came from the darkness. "Let everyone here close his eyes and become blind. He who opens his eyes will be judged a traitor. It is given to only one man to see those who are gathered in this room. Any prying eyes will receive the kiss of a hot iron, that what they have seen may be sealed into the brain."

Leung Fah, seated on the floor, her feet doubled under her, her eyes closed tightly, sensed that men were moving around the room, examining the faces of those who were present by the aid of a flashlight which stabbed its beam into each of the faces. And she could feel heat on her cheeks, which made her realize that a man with a white-hot iron stood nearby ready to plunge the iron into any which might show signs of curiosity.

"She is strange to me," a voice said, a voice which spoke with the hissing sound of the *yut boen gwiee*—the ghosts of the sunrise.

"She is mine," the voice of Sahm Seuh said, and the light ceased to illuminate her closed eyelids. The hot iron passed by.

She heard a sudden scream, the sizzling of a hot iron, a yell of mortal anguish, and the sound of a body as it thudded to the floor. She did not open her eyes. Life, in China, is cheap.

At length the silent roll call had been completed. The voice of Sahm Seuh said, "Eyes may now open."

Leung Fah opened her eyes. The room was black with darkness.

"Shortly before the dawn," Sahm Seuh said, "there will be the roar of many motors in the sky. Each of you will be given a red flare and matches. To each of you will be whispered the name of the place where the red flare is to be placed. When you hear the roar of motors, you will crouch over the flare, as though kneeling on the ground in terror. When the motors reach the eastern end of the city, you will hold a match in your fingers.

"There will be none to watch, because people will be intent on their own safety. When the planes are overhead, you will set fire to the red flares, and then you will run very rapidly. You will return most quickly to this place; you will receive plenty gold.

"It is, however, imperative that you come to this place quickly. The bombing will last until just before daylight. You must be here before the bombing is finished. You will receive your gold. In the confusion you will flee to the river. A boat will be waiting. It will be necessary that you hide for some time, because an investigation will be made. There are spies who spy on us, and one cannot explain the possession of gold. You will be hidden until there is more work to be done."

Once more there was a period of silence, broken only by the shuffling of men and of whispered orders. Leung Fah felt a round wooden object thrust into her hands. A moment later, a box of matches was pushed into her fingers. A man bent over her, so close that his voice breathed a thought directly into her ears, almost without the aid of sound.

"The house of the Commissioner of Public Safety," he said.

The shuffling ceased. The voice of Sahm Seuh said, "That is all. Go, and wait at the appointed places. Hurry back and there will be much gold. In order to avoid suspicion you will leave here one at a time, at intervals of five minutes. A man at the door will control your passing. There will be no lights, no conversation."

Leung Fah stood in the darkness, packed with people whom she did not know, reeking in the stench of stale perspiration. At intervals she heard a whispered command. After each whisper the door would open and one of the persons in that narrow crowded staircase would slip from the suffocating atmosphere into the relative coolness of the street.

At length the door was in front of her. Hands pushed against her. The door swung open and she found herself once more in The Alley of the Sky Horse, shuffling along with demure eyes downcast, and a face which was the face of a sleepwalker.

Leung Fah went only so far as the house where the sacrifices were being offered to the spirit of the departed. The ashes of the sacrificial fire were still smoldering in the narrow street, drifting about in vagrant gusts of wind. Leung Fah knew that in this house there would be mourners, that any who were of the faith and desired to join in sending thought waves to the Ancestor in the Beyond would be welcome.

She climbed the stairs and heard chanting. Around the table were grouped seven nuns with heads as bald as a sharp razor could make them. At another table, flickering peanut-oil lamps illuminated a painting of the ancestor who had in turn joined his ancestors. The table was laden with sacrifices. There were some twenty people in the room who intermittently joined in chanting prayers.

Leung Fah unostentatiously joined this group. Shortly thereafter she moved quietly to the stairs which gave to the roof, and within a half hour had worked her way back to the roof of the house of the three candles. She sought a deep shadow, merged herself within it, and became motionless.

Slowly the hours of the night wore away. Leung Fah began to listen. Her ears, strained toward the east, then heard a peculiar sound. It was like distant thunder over the mountains, a thunder which rumbles ominously.

With terrifying rapidity the murmur of sound in the east grew into a roar. She could hear the screams of people in the streets below, could hear babies, aroused from their sleep as they were snatched up by frantic parents, crying fretfully.

Still Leung Fah remained motionless. The planes swept by overhead. Here and there in the city bright red flares suddenly blossomed into blood-red pools of crimson. And wherever there was a flare, an enemy plane swooped down, and a moment later a mushroom of flame rose up against the night sky, followed by a reverberating report which shook the very foundations of the city.

Leung Fah crept to the edge of the roof where she might peer over and watch The Alley of the Sky Horse. She saw surreptitious figures darting from shadow to shadow, slipping through the portals of the house of three candles.

At length a shadow, more bulky than the rest, the shadow of a fat man running on noiseless feet, crossed the street and was swallowed up in the entrance of the house of three candles. The planes still roared overhead.

Leung Fah placed her box of red fire on the roof and tore off the paper. With calm, untrembling hands, she struck a match to flame, the flame to the flare.

In the crimson pool of light which illuminated all the housetops, Leung Fah fled from one rooftop to another. And yet it seemed she had only been running a few seconds when a giant plane materialized overhead and came roaring down out of the sky. She heard the scream of a torpedo. The entire street rocked under the impact of a stupendous explosion.

Leung Fah was flung to her knees. Her eardrums seemed shattered, her eyes about to burst from their sockets under the enormous rush of pressure which swept along with the blast.

Day was dawning when she recovered enough to limp down to The Alley of the Sky Horse. The roar of the planes was receding into the distance.

Leung Fah hobbled slowly and painfully to the place where the house of the three candles had stood. There was now a deep hole in The Alley of the Sky Horse, a hole surrounded by bits of wreckage and torn bodies.

A blackened torso lay almost at her feet. She examined it intently. It was all that was left of Sahm Seuh.

She turned and limped back up The Alley of the Sky Horse, her eyes downcast and expressionless, her face as though it had been carved of wood.

The sun rose in the east, and the inhabitants of Canton, long since accustomed to having the grim presence of death at their side, prepared to clear away the bodies and debris, to resume once more their daily course of ceaseless activity.

Leung Fah lifted the bamboo yoke to her sore shoulders. *Aiii ah-h-h* it was painful, but one must work if one would eat.

JAYSON BURR AND GABBY HILMAN in

DEATH RIDES
A BOXCAR

When the leg gave its first warning twinge, I stood still for a while and let the rest of the crowd stream on past, up the sloping passenger exit of the big Los Angeles terminal, up to the place where friends and relatives, wives and sweethearts waited in a roped-off space.

It was going to be a job, remembering to favor that leg, but anything was better than hanging around the insipid routine of the hospital.

"Gabby" Hilman was coming by bus. He was to meet me at the Palm Court Hotel around ten o'clock. Until then I was just killing time. I could have started a little celebration over my release from the hospital, but I didn't want to do it without Gabby. He'd been my buddy, and I wanted to start even with him.

There was no such thing as getting a cab to yourself these days. They piled them in two, three, and four at a time. A starter grabbed the light bag I was carrying. "Where to?" he asked.

"Palm Court Hotel."

"Get in."

He held the door open, and that was when I saw class waiting in the cab.

She moved over as I got in. For a moment her eyes rested on mine—large dark eyes that were built to register expression.

I was careful about getting into the cab. "Sorry if I'm a little awkward," I apologized. "I'm nursing a knee back to life."

She smiled, but she didn't say anything.

The cab starter said abruptly, "Where to, sir?" and a man's voice answered, "The corner of Sixth and Figueroa Street."

The cab starter said, "Hop in."

A woman came through the door first, an elderly, white-haired woman with a beaming cheerful face and kindly gray eyes that blinked at me through silver-rimmed spectacles. The man with her looked to be somewhere around 70, so I pulled down the jump seat and moved over. It was rather a slow process because I didn't want to throw the leg out, and I thought the girl on my left watched me with just a little more interest than she'd shown before.

The elderly woman moved over to the middle of the seat, the man got in on the right side. The cab door slammed, and we were off.

It was a short run to Sixth and Figueroa. The man and the woman got off. The girl said to me, "If you're going much farther, you'd better come back to a more comfortable seat."

"Thanks," I told her, and moved back.

Her eyes were solicitous as she watched the way I moved my leg. "Hurt?" she asked.

"It's just a habit," I told her. "It will take some time to get accustomed to throwing the leg around."

She didn't say anything more for a while, and not knowing just how far she was going I decided I'd have to work fast. I took a notebook from my pocket, pulled out a pencil, and said, "I'm an investigator gathering statistics for a Gallup poll. These are questions we have to ask in the line of duty. Have you purchased war bonds?—Not the amount; just yes or no."

She looked at me with a peculiar, half-quizzical expression, and said shortly, "Yes."

"Question Number Two," I went blithely on. "Do you feel sympathetic toward the personnel in the armed forces?"

"Of course."

"Question Number Three. Recognizing the fact that members of the armed forces whom you may encounter are frequently far from home, inclined to be lonely, and with no personal contacts, do you feel it is not only all right, but commendable, to let them make your acquaintance and perhaps, under favorable circumstances, act as your escort for an evening?"

I looked up at her expectantly, holding the pencil poised

over the page.

There was just a twinkle in the dark eyes. "You're asking this question impersonally, of course?"

"Oh, certainly."

"Only as an investigator?"

"That's right."

"Collecting statistics?"

"Correct."

"Therefore, I presume you ask these questions of every woman you encounter who is over eighteen and under thirty?"

She had me there. I saw a bit of triumph in her eyes. "That's not exactly correct," I said.

"Why not?"

"Over *sixteen* and under eighty," I told her, without smiling. "My employers want the field thoroughly covered."

She laughed, and just then the cab made a little lurch as it swung in to the curb over on the left side of the street. "I'm sorry, soldier. Here's where I get off."

"Question Number Four," I said, hurrying the pencil down the page. "Correct name, address, and telephone number."

She just laughed. The cab driver came around and opened the door for her.

"Good night," she said.

I closed the notebook and slipped it back in my pocket. Gabby could probably have done better. He's a whiz at pulling a line out of thin air and getting by with it.

She flashed me a smile. I raised my hat.

In a few minutes we pulled up in front of the Palm Court. I paid the driver and started easing my weight out of the cab.

My hand, resting on the seat cushion, felt something. I looked at it. It was a woman's black leather purse. Returning that purse might give me a chance to begin all over again—starting where I had left off.

I should have said to the cab driver, "That woman left her purse," but there's no use insulting Fortune when she gives a fellow a second chance. I simply slid the purse under my coat and held it there with my elbow.

"Leg bothering you?" the cab driver asked.

"A little stiff, that's all."

The first thing I saw when I opened the purse in my hotel room was a long thin strip of paper about 12 inches long, an inch and a half wide, and covered with a string of figures written with a soft pencil. First was the figure 6, with four straight lines just below it; then the figure 23, four lines, and a tally; then 10 and three lines below that—and so on down the entire strip of paper. On the other side a message had been written in the same soft pencil: "Puzzle No. 2 a little after midnight."

That meant nothing to me, so I placed the strip of paper on the bed and turned so the light would shine into the purse.

There was a wad of greenbacks in there that would have stuffed a sofa cushion.

I felt my heart start pounding as I pulled them out and dumped them on the bed. They were in twenties, fifties, and hundreds, with a small sprinkling of tens and fives.

I started counting. It added up to $7,523 in currency, with a coin purse containing $1.68 in small change.

Then a disquieting thought struck me. The girl who had been in the taxicab had paid her fare when she got to the sidewalk. I distinctly remembered seeing her hand the cab driver the fare. And I was almost certain she was holding an open purse in her hand as she did so—come to think of it, I was certain. This, then, must be the purse that belonged to the white-haired woman.

I started digging down into the lower regions of the purse.

I found a small leather key container which held four keys, then I took out a lipstick, a compact, four cleansing tissues, a small address book of red leather with a loop in front which held a little pencil, and an opened envelope which evidently contained a letter. The envelope was addressed to Muriel Comley, Redderstone Apartments, Los Angeles.

Then I reached for the telephone book.

The voice that answered the telephone sounded very much like that of the girl in the taxicab.

"Is this Muriel Comley?"

An interval—just long enough to be noticeable. Then the smoothly modulated voice said, "Who is this speaking, please?"

"Before I answer," I said, "I'd like to ask you a question. Did you lose something tonight—within the last hour?"

I felt her voice freeze. "I'm sorry, if you can't give me your name, I . . . oh, you mean you've found the purse? Oh!" That last exclamation was filled with sudden dismay. "Will you hold the phone a moment?"

After a while I began to think it was just some sort of runaround. Then she was back.

"Yes. I lost my purse. Do you have it?"

Her voice sounded different from what it had been before—as though her throat had gone dry. I could imagine how she'd feel when she realized she'd lost a wad of dough like that. "I have it," I said, "and it's all safe."

She asked, "Is this, by any chance, the man who is collecting information for the Gallup poll on how women feel toward servicemen?"

"None other."

"I'm so relieved. If you'll just send—"

"I'll deliver it in exactly twelve minutes and thirty seconds," I interpolated, and hung up before she could argue the point.

I found the name Muriel Comley on the list of names to the right of the apartment-house entrance. She was in Apartment 218.

I pressed the bell, and almost immediately the buzzer announced that the door was being unlatched.

I pushed through the door and into the lobby. It wasn't the sort of apartment house in which one would have expected to find a tenant who carried a small fortune in cash in her purse.

I went up to the second floor, found 218, and pressed my finger against the door button.

The girl opened the door, smiling at me with her lips. Her eyes were wide and dark. When she turned so they caught the light, I saw she was afraid. There was terror in those eyes.

Her lips kept smiling. "Won't you come in? I'm sorry I can't offer you a drink, but the apartment seems to be fresh out of drinkables. . . . So you found my purse? It certainly was stupid of me."

I kept the purse under my coat, holding it against my body with my left arm. I said, "I really couldn't believe it was yours."

"Why?"

"I thought you opened a purse when you paid off the cab driver."

She laughed. "Just a coin purse. I happened to have it in my pocket. Do sit down."

I stretched my left leg out in front of me.

"Is it bothering you?" she asked solicitously.

"No. Just habit. . . . Of course, there are certain little formalities. You can describe the purse?"

"Of course. It's black leather with a silver border. The metal at the top has polished silver roses."

"And the contents?"

Her face went blank.

I kept waiting.

"You opened it?"

"Certainly. I had to get your name and address."

She said, "Surely, Mr.—I don't believe I have your name."

"Burr—Jayson Burr."

"Oh, yes. Mr. Burr. Surely you don't doubt that it's my purse," and she was laughing at me now, actually making me feel uncomfortable.

"I'm afraid you're going to have to describe the contents."

"Well, let me see. There was my lipstick, my compact, and—yes, I left my keys in there."

"Have any trouble getting into the apartment?" I asked casually, and watched her.

She said, without batting an eyelash, "I always keep a duplicate key in my pocket. I've lost my purse before. I'm a bit absent-minded."

"All right. So far we've got lipstick, compact, and keys. What else?"

"Isn't that enough?"

"I'm afraid that's too general an inventory. It would describe the contents of any woman's purse."

"Well, let's see," she said archly, as though playing some very interesting game. "Since I'm accused of stealing my own purse—or *am* I accused of stealing it?"

"No accusation," I smiled, "no stealing. Simply for my own protection."

"That's right; you *are* entitled to some protection. Well, let's see. There was my address book in there, and some cleansing tissues, and—and a coin purse."

"Can you tell me how much money?"

"I'm sorry, I simply can't. I always carry an extra coin purse in my pocket. Sort of mad money, you know, and then carry the balance in—oh, I suppose there's ten or twelve dollars probably, altogether, but I can't be certain at all."

"And was there anything else?" I asked.

She frowned. "Really, Mr. Burr, I can't remember *all* the little details. Surely I've identified the purse well enough. . . . You have it with you?"

I looked her squarely in the eyes and lied like a trooper. "I decided I'd better leave it in the hotel until you'd identified it."

"Why, what a strange way to—" she broke off and looked puzzled, a frown furrowing her forehead.

"I'm sorry," I said, "but, you see, you failed to describe the most important thing that was in the purse."

She was silent for a matter of seconds, then, abruptly, she got to her feet. "Mr. Burr, I've tried to be patient. I've tried to make allowances. But don't you think that, in the first place, you should have returned the purse to the cab driver? In the second place, you should have carried your investigation of the contents of the purse only far enough to have ascertained my name and address. In the third place, I *have* described the purse to you—in the greatest detail."

"The exterior."

"The exterior!" she repeated with icy dignity. "And that should be enough in dealing with a *gentleman*."

I just grinned at her.

She said angrily, "You know I *could* have you arrested for taking that purse."

"Why don't you? Then I'll tell the judge to turn it over to you just as soon as you've described the contents."

"That wouldn't help *you* any."

"I don't know much law, but I think you'd have to convince a jury that it was *your* purse before you could convict me of stealing it, wouldn't you?"

Suddenly she was sarcastic. "Very well, if *that's* the way you feel about it I would prefer to lose the purse than put up with your insolence."

She swept toward the door and held it open.

That wasn't the way I had planned the interview to go at all. "Look here," I said. "All I want is a reasonable assurance that—"

"Thank you, Mr. Burr," she interrupted. "All I want is my purse. You admit that you came over here without it. Therefore, no matter *what* I may say, you can't deliver my purse to me here and now. Under the circumstances I see no use in prolonging the discussion. I will say this, that if you don't have that purse in my hands before tomorrow morning I'll have you arrested."

"You can have your purse just as soon as you—"

"I don't care to discuss it any more."

She was watching me as I stood holding my left arm against my side. She must have realized that the purse was under my coat, but she said nothing.

I walked out of the door and said, "Good night," without looking back. I heard the vicious slam of the door.

I was halfway to the elevator before I was aware she was following me.

The elevator was waiting there at the second floor. I pulled the door open and stepped to one side for her to get in.

She walked in ahead of me, chin up, eyes cold. I got in, closed the door, and pushed the button for the ground floor.

Neither one of us said anything.

The cage rattled to a stop. I opened the door, waited for her to get out. She was careful not to touch me as she walked past.

A man was sitting at the horseshoe desk behind a sign reading MANAGER. He was a narrow-shouldered chap with thick-lensed spectacles which gave his face a look of studious abstraction. He blinked owlishly in my general direction, and then lowered his eyes to a daybook in which he was making some entries.

The girl cleared her throat loudly, then said, "Pardon me."

The man at the desk looked up.

When she was sure his eye was on her, she grabbed for my left arm, which was holding the purse firmly against my body on the inside of my coat.

I was ready for her, and lowered my shoulder.

Her body struck against the shoulder and glanced off. Her hands clawed at my coat.

The clerk at the desk said, in mildly bewildered reproof, "Come, come, we can't have—"

The girl hung onto me. "Will you please call the police! This man has stolen my purse!"

The clerk blinked.

I smiled at him and said, "I've found *a* purse. She *says* it's hers, but she can't identify it."

She said to the clerk indignantly, "I've described it in detail. Please do as I say. Call the police!"

The clerk looked at me, then looked at her rather dubiously. "You're with Mrs. Comley?" he asked. "Aren't you the lady who just moved in?"

That question did it. She was licked the minute he asked her that question.

The clerk seemed surprised by her sudden surrender. "Oh, all *right*," she stormed. "Take the purse if you think it will do you any good." She flounced toward the elevator.

I raised my hat. "Good evening," I said, and walked out.

I was dozing in the hotel lobby and didn't see Gabby when he came in. The first I knew, I woke up with a start, and there he was looking down with that good-natured grin of his.

"Hi, soldier," he said.

I came up out of the chair, forgetting everything the doc

had told me about the leg. Gabby thumped me on the shoulder and I made a quick pass at his chin. Then we shook hands.

We went up to the room. Gabby splashed around in the bathtub and I told him all about the purse.

"Where you got this purse now?" Gabby asked.

"I did it up in a bundle and told the hotel clerk that the package contained important military documents, to put it in a safe, and to be darn sure no one else got it."

Gabby, pulling clean clothes out of his bag, thought things over while he got dressed. "This jane is class?" he asked.

"With a capital C."

"Why wouldn't she tell you what was in the bag?"

"She didn't know. She isn't Muriel Comley."

"Then what was she doing in Muriel Comley's apartment?"

"I don't know. Seemed like she was visiting, from what the clerk said."

"Seems like we'd ought to do something about this," Gabby said, and winked.

"That's the way I felt."

"Maybe Muriel's good-looking," Gabby suggested.

"Could be."

"What," Gabby asked, "are we waiting for?"

"You."

Gabby grinned, struggled into his coat, and said, "Let's go."

At the apartment-house entrance I rang the bell of 218 and we stood there waiting, tingling with that feeling of excitement which comes from doing something interesting and not being quite certain what is going to happen next. After a few seconds I pressed the button again. When there was still no answer I said to Gabby, "Perhaps she's been expecting this and decided nothing doing."

"Perhaps she's gone to bed."

I said, "Oh, well then, we wouldn't want to get her up. Oh, no! We'll go right on back to the hotel."

Gabby laughed.

I moved over to the front door, pressed my face against the glass, looked inside, holding my hands up at the side of my face to shut out the reflection of the street lights. There was no one at the desk. The lobby looked deserted.

"Anything doing?" Gabby asked.

"No. Evidently the clerk's gone to bed and this outer door is kept locked at night."

I pressed a couple of other buttons. On my second try the buzzer on the door whirred, and Gabby, pushing against the door, stumbled in as the door opened. We walked up the one flight of stairs.

Just as I raised my hand to knock on the door of 218, Gabby caught my wrist. Then I saw that the door lacked about a sixteenth of an inch of being closed. The apartment was dark behind it and from where I was standing, the door looked to be securely closed. Standing over at Gabby's angle, you could see it wasn't.

We stood there for a second or two in silence, looking at the door. Then Gabby pushed the door open.

I went in. We found the light switch, snapped on the lights, and Gabby heeled the door shut behind us.

The apartment was just as I had last seen it. Nothing seemed to have been touched or moved.

Gabby tried a door which led to a kitchenette. While Gabby was prowling around in there, I opened the other door.

"Gabby!" I yelled.

Gabby's heels pounded the floor, and his fingers dug into my shoulder as we stood looking at what lay there on the bed.

The body was sprawled in that peculiarly awkward position which is the sign of death. By the weird, unreal light cast by a violet globe in the bed lamp I could see his features. I had the feeling I'd seen him before, and recently too. Then I remembered. "It's the clerk at the desk downstairs," I said.

Gabby gave a low whistle, moved around the end of the bed, paused, looking down at the floor.

"Don't touch it," I warned as I saw him bend over. I moved around and joined him, looking down at the thing on the floor lying near the side of the bed.

It was a club some two feet long, square at one end, round at the other, and covered with sinister stains which showed black in the violet light. There were three rings cut in the billet, up near the round end, and, between these rings were crosses; first a cross like a sign of addition, then a conventional cross with a horizontal arm two-thirds of the way up the perpendicular, then another cross of addition.

We searched the rest of the place. No one was there.

"I think," I said, "someone's putting in too many chips for us to sit in the game."

"Looks like it to me," Gabby admitted.

We left the door slightly ajar, just as we had found it. We couldn't be bothered with the elevator, but went tiptoeing down the corridor at a constantly accelerating rate. I wanted to get out of the place.

Suddenly down at the far end of the corridor a dog barked twice. Those two short barks made me jump half out of my clothes and sent a chill up my spine. Gabby moved right along. I doubt if he even heard them. . . .

We didn't say any more all the way to the hotel. We went up to our room. Gabby sat down in the big chair by the window and lit a cigarette. I pulled up my bag and started scooping up the stuff on the bed and cramming it in. When I had my clean clothes packed, I spread out my soiled shirt so I could wrap clothes in it for the laundry. A slip of paper fluttered to the floor.

"What's that?" Gabby asked.

I picked it up. "That's the piece of paper that was in the purse. I put stuff from the purse out on the bed, and I'd also dumped my bag—"

"Let's see it."

I handed it over.

Gabby frowned. " 'Puzzle No. 2 a little after midnight.' That mean anything, Jay?"

"Not to me."

Gabby's eyes were cold and hard. "Never heard of a switch list—or a puzzle switch?"

"No." I knew then, just from the way Gabby was looking

at me, that we were in for something.

"You see, Jay, there's just a chance this is a trap we're being invited to walk into."

"Sort of will-you-walk-into-my-parlor-asked-the-spider-of-the-fly?" I inquired inanely.

"Exactly."

"So what do we do?"

Gabby's lips were a thin line. "We walk in. Come on, Jay. We're going to the freight yards. I have to see a man down there anyway, and this is as good a time as any."

We got across the yards in a series of jerks and dashes to a big wooden building. Gabby led me up a flight of stairs, down a long corridor lined with offices, and pushed open a door.

A man who had been writing down figures on the page of a book glanced up. An expression of annoyance gave way to astonishment. Then the swivel chair went swirling back on its casters as he jumped to his feet.

"You old son of a gun!" the man exclaimed.

Gabby gave that slow grin of his and said, "Fred, this is Jay Burr," and to me, jerking his head toward the man in the green eyeshade, "Fred Sanmore."

Just then a train came rumbling through and it sounded as though the building was within a half mile or so of a heavy bombardment. Everything shook and trembled. The roar of sound filled the room so there was no chance to talk. We simply sat there and waited.

When the train had passed, Sanmore went back of the desk, took off his eyeshade, and said to Gabby, "You old so and so, you want something."

"How did you know?" Gabby asked.

"Because I know you. You're here on furlough. This is your first night in town. You've been here for a couple of hours. By this time you'd be buying drinks for a blonde, a brunette, and a redhead—if you didn't want something. What is it?"

Gabby pulled the strip of paper out of his pocket. "List of cars going past the puzzle switch?" he asked.

"Probably coming on a switch from over the hump."

"What," I asked, "is a hump?"

Sanmore started to answer me, then turned to Gabby instead. "Why do you want to know, Gabby?"

"Just checking up."

Sanmore sighed and turned back to me. "Sorry, Burr. A hump is the high point on a two-way incline. You push cars up to the hump, then cut 'em loose, and gravity takes 'em down across the yards. It saves a lot of wear and tear, a lot of steam, releases a lot of rolling stock, and handles a cut a lot faster than you can any other way."

"And a cut?" I asked.

He grinned. "Any number of freight cars taken from a train switched around yards. Even if it's a whole train. The minute a switch engine gets hold of it, it's a cut."

Gabby said, "Any idea whose figures these are?"

Sanmore shook his head. "We might be able to find out."

"You're certain that's what this list is?" I asked.

"Positive."

"Would it be too much to ask just what makes you certain?"

He said, "Well, in the first place, notice the numbers. There aren't any of them higher than ninety-seven. We have ninety-seven numbers on our terminal card index. Whenever a train comes in, a switch list is made up, and numbers are put on the cars for different destinations.

"For instance, here's Number One, and underneath it are three lines. That means there are three cars in a row for T N O Manifest. Then here's two lines under Number Eleven. That means two cars in a row for Indio. Then there are two lines under the figure four, which means two successive cars for the El Paso Manifest.

"Now then, loosen up and tell me what brings you two goofs in here at this hour of the night to ask questions about railroading."

Gabby said awkwardly, "Just got curious, that was all. Jay thought it might be a code."

Sanmore kept looking at Gabby.

Gabby reached for the strip of paper.

Sanmore started to hand it to him, then idly turned it over.

Gabby grabbed for it.

Sanmore jerked his hand back and read the message on the back: "'Puzzle No. 2 a little after midnight.'" I saw his eyebrows get level.

Gabby didn't say anything.

Sanmore slid down off the corner of the desk. "Come on, you birds."

He led the way down the stairs, out through a door, and up along the tracks bearing off to the left.

"This is a bit tricky," Sanmore said, as the tracks began to converge. "Watch your step along here." Abruptly he reached out, grabbed our arms. "Hold it!"

I couldn't see what had stopped us, when all at once a great bulk loomed out of the night. It was so close and seemed so ominously massive I wanted to jump back, but Sanmore's grip held me. And I realized then that another big shape was moving along just behind me.

"Putting cars over the hump," Sanmore explained.

As the car passed I could hear the sound of its wheels rumbling over the steel rails. But its approach had been as quiet as though I had been in the jungle and some huge elephant had come padding softly up behind me.

"All right," Sanmore said, and we went forward again.

"This is dangerous," Sanmore said. "You get one of those big boxcars rolling along by gravity and it's like a fifty-ton steel ball moving slowly down an incline. You can't stop 'em; you can't turn 'em. They don't have any whistle or any bell. They don't make very much noise against the background noise from the yards, particularly when they're coming toward you. . . . Okay; here we are, boys. Here's one of the puzzle switches."

A man sat at a complicated switch mechanism, a slip of narrow paper in his hands similar to the one I had found in Muriel Comley's purse. A seemingly endless stream of cars was rolling down the tracks that fed into the intricate mechanism of the switch—a remorselessly steady procession which called for carefully coordinated thought and action.

Sanmore said, "He's too busy to talk now. Let's go find the hump foreman."

We started moving up the tracks. I paused as I saw a

line of men seated by a stretch of track. In front of them was a string of holes and in many of these holes there were billets of hickory, substantial clubs some two feet or more in length, identical, as nearly as I could tell, with the club we had seen on the floor by the murdered man.

Sanmore answered my unspoken question. "These are the men who ride the cars down," he said. "The hump is back up here. We put the cars over the hump. The pinmen uncouple the cars in units according to the numbers on them. Then one of these boys—notice that chap on the end now."

Two cars came rumbling down the track. A man swung lazily up out of a chair, picked up one of the hickory clubs, stood for a moment by the track gauging the speed of the oncoming cars, then swung casually up the iron ladder, climbed to the brake wheel, inserted his billet to give leverage on the wheel, tightened it enough to get the feel of the brakes, and then clung to the car, peering out into the darkness.

The car moved onward, seeming neither to gather speed nor to slow down as it moved. The man at the puzzle switch flipped a little lever. The car rattled across switch frogs, turned to the left, and melted away into the darkness.

A stocky competent man, who looked hard and seemed to have a deep scorn for anything that wasn't as hard and as tough as he was, came walking down the track.

Sanmore said, "Cuttering, couple of friends of mine looking the ground over. . . . Whose figures are these?"

The man took one look at the long list of figures on the slip of paper; he looked at Sanmore, then he looked at Gabby, and finally at me.

"They're *my* figures," he said in a voice that had an edge of truculence. "What about it?"

Silently Sanmore turned over the slip and showed Cuttering the writing on the back.

"Not my writing," Cuttering said.

"Know whose it is?"

"No."

"Any idea what this message means?"

"No. Look here; there's a half a dozen of these old lists lying along the tracks. We throw 'em away after a cut has gone over the hump and through the switches. Anyone who wanted to write a message to someone and wanted a piece of paper to write it on could pick up one of these slips."

There was an uneasy silence for half a minute.

"What's so important about this?" Cuttering asked sharply.

"It may be evidence."

"Of what?"

I met the steady hostility of his eyes. "I don't know."

I reached for the strip of paper. "You'll have to make a copy of it," I said. "This one is evidence."

Wordlessly, while we watched, Cuttering copied off the string of numbers with the lines underneath them. Then, just before he reached the end, he frowned and said, "Wait a minute. We put this through yesterday night about eleven fifteen."

Sanmore didn't waste any more time. His voice was packed with the authority of a man giving an order. "Get me everything you have on that, Bob." Then he turned to Gabby. "We'll check those cars through the Jumbo Book, Gabby, if you think it's that important."

Gabby said simply, "I think it's that important. We're at the Palm Court. You can phone us there."

Gabby said to the cab driver, "Go a little slow in the next block, will you? I want to take a look on the side street."

The driver obligingly slowed. "This the place you want?" he called back.

"Next street," Gabby said, swinging around to look at the Redderstone Apartments.

Then Gabby and I exchanged puzzled looks. The apartments were dark. The street in front showed no activity. There was no unusual congestion of vehicles parked at the curb.

"Okay?" the driver asked as he crawled past the next side street.

"Okay," I said.

We went on to the Palm Court, paid off the cab driver,

stood for a moment on the sidewalk. Neither of us wanted to go in.

"What do you make of it?" Gabby asked in a low voice.

I said, "We've got to tip off the police."

"We'll be in bad if we do it now."

"We've got to do it, Gabby."

"You don't think the police have been notified, cleaned up the place, and gone?"

I didn't even bother to answer.

"Okay," Gabby said. "Let's go."

We went into the lobby, nodded to the clerk on duty, and I walked over to the telephone booth. Gabby stood by the door until I motioned him away so I could close the door tightly.

I dialed police headquarters and said, "This is the Redderstone Apartments. Did you get a call about some trouble up here—about an hour and a half ago?"

"Just a minute," the voice said at the other end of the line. "I'll check with the broadcasting department. . . . What was it about?"

I said, "You'll find it all right—if it's there."

"Okay. Just a minute."

I held onto the line while the receiver made little singing noises in my ear. Then the voice said, "No, we haven't anything from the Redderstone Apartments. Why? What's the trouble?"

"Apartment two-eighteen," I said, "has a murdered man. You should have known about it an hour ago," and hung up.

Gabby was waiting for me in the lobby. His brows raised in a question.

"They know nothing about it."

"You reported it?"

I nodded.

Gabby and I went over to the desk to get the key.

The clerk took a memo out of the box, along with the key. "Some young woman's been trying to get to you. She waited here nearly half an hour."

"A good-looking brunette with large dark eyes," I asked, "about twenty-two or twenty-three, good figure?"

94

"Easy on the eyes," he said somewhat wistfully, "but she isn't a brunette. She's a redhead, blue eyes, dark red hair—guess you'd call it auburn. A quick-stepping little number."

"She didn't leave any name?"

"No name."

"Want to wait?" I asked Gabby.

He said, for the clerk's benefit, "Time was when I'd have waited all night on a hundred-to-one chance a girl like that would come back, but now I want shut-eye."

"Same here," I told him.

We went up in the elevator and hadn't much more than unlocked the door of the room when the telephone rang.

I picked up the receiver, and the voice of the clerk, who was evidently taking over the switchboard on the night shift, said, "She's here again. Wants to come up."

"Send her up," I told him, hung up the phone, and said to Gabby, "A redheaded gal is about to cross our paths."

Gabby walked over to the mirror, hitched his tie into position, ran a comb through his wavy hair. "Let's not fire until we see the whites of her eyes. Perhaps she has a friend."

Knuckles tapped with gentle impatience against the panel of the door.

I opened it.

The girl was something to take pictures of and then pin the pictures up on the wall.

"Won't you come in?" I asked.

She walked in as easily and naturally as though this was where she lived. She took off her gloves, smiled affably up at me, and said, "Which one of you is Mr. Burr?"

I nodded. "I have the—"

"Honor," Gabby finished.

We all laughed then and the tension let down. She said casually, "I'm Muriel Comley."

"*You* are!"

The blue eyes widened in surprise. "Why, yes. Why not?"

I said, "You aren't the Muriel Comley I saw earlier."

She looked puzzled for a minute, and then said, "Oh, you must have seen Lorraine."

"Who's Lorraine?"

"Lorraine Dawson."

"Tell me a little more about Lorraine."

"Lorraine was looking for an apartment on a fifty-fifty basis. I had this place on a lease. It was too big for me, and too much rent. Lorraine came in with me about a week ago."

I said, "You might tell me how it happens Lorraine got hold of your purse."

"She didn't get hold of it. I merely left it in the taxi. I got out. Lorraine stayed in."

"And how did you know where to come for your purse?"

"The taxi driver said you had it."

I raised my eyebrows.

"You see," she said, "I called up the cab company. The purse hadn't been turned in. They got hold of the cab driver. He said he remembered you had picked something up from the seat of the cab when you got out. He thought it might have been the purse."

"I didn't know you had been in that cab."

She sighed. "Lorraine and I went to the depot," she explained. "I got out and went to meet a train. Lorraine was coming on home, and wasn't going to wait. I waited down there at the depot for the train to come in. The person I expected to meet wasn't on it. Then suddenly I realized I didn't have my purse. I thought back, and remembered that I must have left it in the cab. That was when I called the cab company. Now do I have to explain to you anything more about my private affairs in order to get what belongs to me? After all, Mr. Burr, your own actions are subject to considerable question."

Gabby said, "He's just trying to be sure, that's all."

She turned to him, and her eyes softened into a smile.

I said, "I'm not interested in your private affairs. But, under the circumstances, since you're the second person this evening who has claimed to be Muriel Comley, I'd like some proof."

"Very well," she said, dropped her hand to the pocket of her light coat, and pulled out a transparent envelope which contained a driver's license.

The driver's license was made out to Muriel Comley. The description fit her to a T.

"The purse," she said, "is of black leather with a smooth glossy finish. The mountings are silver with narrow borders stamped around the edges of the metal, silver curlicues embossed against a dull-finished background. The handles are of braided leather. Is that enough?"

"The contents?"

"You looked inside?"

"Naturally."

She met my eyes. "The purse," she said, "contained something over seven thousand five hundred dollars in cash, in addition to having my lipstick, keys, a small coin purse with about a dollar and a half in change, an embroidered handkerchief, some cleansing tissues, an address book, and a compact."

Gabby sighed. "I guess," he said to me, "she gets the purse."

I hesitated.

"Well?" she demanded.

"All right," I said.

At length, after I had signed my name on a receipt, being at the receiving end of suspicious scrutiny from the clerk, the package was returned to me.

Back in the apartment I unwrapped the purse, handed it to her, and said, "Please count the money."

She opened the purse, took out the money, spread the bills on the floor, and counted them carefully. Then she said, "Thank you, Mr. Burr," snapped the purse shut, and started for the door.

Gabby opened it for her. Her eyes caressed his. "Thank you very much, Mr. Hilman," she said, and was gone.

I stood looking after her. "I don't like it," I said.

"For the love of Mike, Jay! Snap out of it! She owns the purse. You've got her address. You—"

"And there's a murdered man in her apartment."

"Well, what of it? You can see she doesn't know anything about it."

"Don't be too certain," I said.

I was just getting into bed, and Gabby, in his pajamas,

was sitting on the edge of the chair smoking a last cigarette, when knuckles tapped on the door.

Gabby looked at me in surprise.

Suddenly I remembered. "She's back after that slip of paper, I bet."

"My gosh!" Gabby said. "You got a robe, Jay?"

"Gosh, no," I told him. "You're decent. Go to the door."

"What do you mean I'm decent?" Gabby demanded, looking down at his pajamas.

The light tapping on the door was resumed. "Stick your head out if you're so damned modest," I said. "After all, she's been married. She must know what pajamas are. Tell her you're going to get dressed and take her down to a cocktail bar."

"*That's* an idea!" Gabby barefooted across to the door, opened it a scant three inches, cleared his throat, and said, in the very dulcet tone he reserved for particularly good-looking women, "I'm sorry—you see, I was just getting into bed. I—"

The door pushed open as though a steam roller had been on the other end of it. Gabby jumped up in the air, grabbed his left big toe, and started hopping around in agonized circles.

A tall competent-looking man in a gray suit, a gray hat to match, with a face that was lean and bronzed, pushed his way into the room and slammed the door shut behind him.

Gabby managed to sidetrack the pain of his skinned toe long enough to get belligerent. "Say," he demanded, "who the hell do you think *you* are? Get out of here, and—"

"Now then," the man announced, "what kind of a damn racket are you two guys pulling?"

"And just who are you?" I asked.

"Inspector Fanston, Headquarters. What's the idea?"

"The idea of what?"

"Who was the jane who was just up in the room?"

I said, "I'm not going to lie to you, Inspector. Her mother and I are estranged and she came to get me to go home. But I told her nothing doing. I shouldn't have married a woman who was forty-five years older than I was in the first place, and I should never have had a daughter who was only five years younger. It makes for a terrific strain on family life. Or don't you think so?"

"Do you," he asked, "think this is a gag?"

"Why not? We're over twenty-one. And if a woman can't pay us a five-minute visit in a hotel room without some house dick—"

"Forget it. I'm not a house dick. I'm from headquarters. I want to know who the woman was, and when you get done making wisecracks I want to know what the hell the idea was ringing up headquarters and telling them a murder had been committed at the Redderstone Apartments."

Neither Gabby nor I said anything for a minute.

The Inspector grinned, settled down on the edge of the bed, and said, "That makes it different, doesn't it, wise guy?"

"That makes it very much different," I told him. "How—how did you—?"

"Easy," he said. "When the desk sergeant told you he was consulting with the broadcasting system he was tracing the call. The hotel clerk remembered you going in to telephone, and there's been a cute little number dropping in. . . . What the hell's the idea? What are you two guys trying to do?"

I cleared my throat. "About the purse," I said.

"Let's talk about the murder first, if you don't mind."

I said, "I—er—thought—"

"Did you?" he interrupted. "Well, try thinking it out straight this time. I suppose you boys are on the loose for a little night life, and it's okay by me just so you don't start pulling practical jokes about murders."

"Practical jokes!" I exclaimed. "A man had the back of his head caved in."

"What man?"

"The man in 218 at the Redderstone Apartments."

He said, "Get up and get your clothes on," and nodded to Gabby. "You too."

We went to the Redderstone Apartments and up to the second floor. An officer in uniform was on guard in the living room of 218. The bedroom was just as we had left it, except now the bed was a spotless expanse of smooth counterpane.

I had been bracing myself for the shock of being called on to identify the body—perhaps being accused of having had something to do with the crime, and wondering just how I could establish an alibi. But the sight of that smooth bed was too much for me. I stood there for a good two or three seconds.

"Any old time," Fanston said.

Gabby and I both started talking at once. Then Gabby quit and let me tell the story. I knew there was only one thing to do. I told it right from the beginning, with the uniformed cop looking at me skeptically and Fanston's eyes drilling tunnels right into my brain.

"You *sure* this was the apartment?"

"Absolutely."

Inspector Fanston didn't give up. "All right, let's concede that he looked dead—that you thought he was dead. Those things don't just happen, you know."

"It happened this time."

"Wait a minute until you see what I'm getting at. Suppose it was all planned. A purse is planted where you'll be certain to find it. There's enough money in it so you'll really start doing something about it. It's a foregone conclusion that you're coming to this apartment—not once, but twice. And the second time you come back you find the outer door open. A man is lying sprawled on the bed. There's a violet-colored bulb in the lamp over the bed. That would make anyone look dead as a doornail.

"My best guess is that it's either some new racket or a frame-up to get you two guys on a spot because you two guys just happen to be you two guys. If it's a racket, you look old enough to take care of yourselves. If either one of you has any particular military information, or is here on some secret mission—well, I think that now would be a good time to take the police into your confidence."

He looked at Gabby. "Right, soldier?"

Gabby just looked innocent. Then he took a leather case from his pocket and handed it to the Inspector. "Keep it to yourself," he said.

The Inspector turned his back. I saw slight motion in his shoulders as he opened the leather case. Then he was motionless and silent for a few seconds.

I heard the snap of a catch, and the Inspector turned, poker-faced.

He handed the leather case back to Gabby.

"Then you don't think there really was anybody?" I asked.

Fanston said, "Hell, no. Now, go home. If you start buzzing these janes in the morning, be careful—that's all."

Gabby snorted.

"They're so dumb they think they've fooled us. Do you want to go back to the hotel now, Jay?"

"No. Let's find out some more about that stick—and what's happening at Puzzle Number Two shortly after midnight."

We found Fred Sanmore still on duty, tired to the point of utter weariness, but still shoving traffic through the yards.

"Look, Fred," Gabby said, "those brake sticks the men use—does it make any difference which is which?"

"What do you mean?"

"Can any man pick up any stick?"

Sanmore laughed. "Gosh, no. That's a sure way to pick a fight. Each man has his own stick. When a shift comes on duty, they'll bundle up all of the sticks and heave them out as far as they can throw them. The man whose stick goes the farthest puts it in the last hole. He's the last one out."

"How do they tell them apart?"

"Oh, various markings."

Gabby said, with what seemed to me just a little too much innocence, "I don't suppose you happen to know who owns the stick that has three rings out near the end with a series of crosses between the rings?"

"No, but I can find out for you."

"If you could do it quietly," Gabby said, "so your inquiries didn't attract too much attention, that might help."

"Come on," Sanmore said.

We started up toward the place where the men were sitting in front of the line of pegs. There weren't so many of them now. The cut that was going over the hump was getting down to the last ten or fifteen cars.

Sanmore left us and talked with two or three of the switchmen in a low voice, then was back to say, "As nearly as I can tell, it's a man named Carl Greester. He went off duty at midnight, but he's still around somewhere. He has a friend visiting him in the yards."

"What do you mean, a friend?"

Sanmore grinned. "I mean a *friend*," and holding up his hands in front of him he made an hourglass outline of a woman's figure. "She came down with a pass from headquarters. And she had another woman with her. Greester is having a confab with them."

"You don't know where Greester lives, do you?" I asked.

"Gosh, no. But I can find out."

"Look, Fred," Gabby said suddenly. "Could Jay and I ride one of these cars down to its destination, just to see what it's like?"

"Absolutely against the rules," Sanmore told him brusquely. "If I saw you do it, I'd have to jerk you off the car and have you put out of the yards." And then he deliberately walked away.

A big freight car came lumbering down the incline. One of the switchmen, moving with lazy coordination, picked up his stick and swung aboard the front of the car.

Gabby and I, acting just as though we had received formal permission from the foreman, walked over to the back ladder.

"You first," Gabby said.

I favored the leg as much as possible, taking it easy up to the top of the car.

"Hang on," Gabby said, as his head came up over the edge of the boxcar. I looked ahead and saw we were right on the puzzle switch, and braced myself, expecting that I would be thrown from one side to the other as the trucks went over the frogs; but the big loaded car moved along in majestic dignity. There was only a little jar as the wheels underneath us made noise. Then we were gliding out from the well-lighted area into the half-darkness, then out to where it was completely dark.

We clicked over a couple of other switches, then veered sharply to the right and were coasting along when I heard a scream coming from almost directly beneath the car.

Gabby was where he could look down on the side. Then he was climbing down the ladder. "Come on, Jay!"

I looked back and caught a glimpse of two girls. A man was with them. Evidently he'd put his arms around them and jerked them back out of the way of the car.

I forgot all about the leg as I came down the iron ladder, but Gabby was running alongside and eased me to the ground on that last jump.

My knee gave me a little twinge just as we passed a couple of boxcars on a track on the left. I dropped back and said, "Go ahead, Gabby. I'll catch up."

Gabby turned to look at me, and then I saw him stiffen. At what I saw on his face I forgot about the leg and whirled.

Three men, armed with brake sticks, were right on top of us. A year ago I'd have been frightened into giving ground and making useless motions, but I'd learned a lot since then. The man who was nearest me raised his club. I shot my left straight to the Adam's apple. I saw Gabby pivot sideways to let a blow slide harmlessly past him, grab the man's wrist, give the arm a swift wrench, then heave. The air became filled with arms and legs as the man went flying through the darkness, to crash against the side of a boxcar, then drop limply to the ground.

The man I had hit was on the ground. He made a wild swing at my shins with the brake stick. Automatically, and without thinking, I tried to jump back out of the way. The injured knee gave way without warning. Then the brake stick cracked against my shin and I went down on my knees. Suddenly I lost balance and fell forward. As I fell I spread apart the first and second fingers of my right hand and jabbed the fingers toward his eyes. If he wanted to play dirty I could teach him something about that. I'd specialized in it.

I heard a faint swish. Something—perhaps the sixth sense which wild things have and which we develop under the spur of life-and-death conflict—warned me. I jerked my head to one side, but not soon enough and not far enough. . . .

The next thing I remembered, I was in a warm musty darkness with a sore head and an aching sensation at my wrists. I tried to move my arms, and realized my hands were tied behind my back.

From the stuffy thick blackness I heard Gabby's voice. "How's it coming, Jay?"

"What," I asked, "happened?"

"The guy from behind," Gabby explained. "The one who was with the two girls. He caught you on the head just as you went down. I smeared his nose all over his face with a straight right., and then the guy behind me hit me just over the kidneys with everything he had."

"What about the girls?"

Gabby said, "The redhead ran away. I think she's gone for help. The other one just stood there watching. The damn spy."

My head was feeling a little better, although it still ached.

I said, "If you ask me, it was the redhead who was the decoy. They wouldn't have let her run away if she hadn't been. Where are we?"

"Inside a boxcar."

"What," I asked, "is it all about?"

Once more Gabby was silent, but this time it was the tight-lipped silence of a man who is carefully guarding a secret.

I tried to roll over so I could take some of the pressure off my wrists. My shoulder hurt and it was hard to keep my balance.

Gabby heard me move.

"Take it easy, Jay. I'm getting this knot worked loose, I think."

After a minute or two Gabby said triumphantly, "I've got it, Jay. Just another minute and we'll be loose, and then we'll be out of here."

I heard his feet on the planks, heard him starting toward me—

With an ominous rumble the door slid back along its tracks. The beam of a flashlight stabbed into the darkness.

Gabby flung himself flat on the floor, keeping his ankles crossed, his hands behind his back.

There was a peculiar scuffling sound from the outer darkness, then the sobbing breathing of a woman.

I got my head around to where I could see a little more of what was happening.

Lorraine Dawson was literally lifted and thrown into the car by the three men.

The beam of the flashlight swung around and then suddenly stopped. "Do you," demanded a voice, "see what I see?"

I looked along the beam of the flashlight. It was centered on the pieces of rope that Gabby had untied from his wrists and ankles.

The three men were bunched there in the doorway, the beam of the flashlight holding Gabby as a target like a helpless airplane caught in a vortex of searchlights.

Gabby made one swift leap and hit the group feet first.

I heard the thud of his heels striking against flesh. The flashlight was jerked up, looped the loop, hit the side of the boxcar, hesitated a moment at the edge of the door, then fell to the tracks. The sounds of bodies threshing around in a struggle, the thud of blows filled the night. All of a sudden there was a lull, then shouts and curses as our assailants piled out of the boxcar. Good old Gabby had given them the slip and was leading them away.

Almost immediately the rumbling noise from the trucks indicated that the car had been banged into rapid motion. The door was still open. I could feel the fresh night air coming in through the opening to eddy around the interior of the boxcar.

"You all right?" I asked the girl.

"Yes. . . . Who are you?"

"Believe it or not, I'm Jayson Burr, who wanted to return the purse you lost. That was when you were masquerading as Muriel Comley. Remember?"

I heard the quick intake of her breath. "How did *you* get here?" she demanded.

"It's a long story. Would you mind telling me just what your name really is?"

"I'm Lorraine," she said.

"And who's Muriel?"

"Believe it or not, I don't know. About all I do know is that she had an attractive apartment and wanted a room-mate to share expenses. I moved in."

I swung around and managed to get into a sitting position.

"Would you," I asked, "mind telling me something of what this is all about?"

"I don't know."

"Then perhaps you can tell me why you don't know."

She said, "I only moved in with Muriel a few days ago. She seemed nice, and just recently secured a divorce. To-night Muriel was to meet someone who was due to come in on a train. I don't even know whether it was a man or a woman. We were in town. I wanted to take a cab to the apartment, so I dropped Muriel at the depot. They said the cab had to take on a full load before it started back. You know the rest. I never realized Muriel had left her purse until she telephoned me at the apartment; then, just after she'd hung up, you telephoned."

The cars were rattling and banging over switches, lurching crazily.

"And then you said *you* were Muriel?"

"Yes, of course. I didn't know who you were, but you had Muriel's purse, and I wanted to get it back for her. I thought it was easier to pretend to be Muriel than to do a lot of explaining, and then have you insist on waiting for Muriel to come back to claim the purse."

"And when I got up there," I said, "you were frightened."

"I'll tell the world I was frightened."

"Can you tell me what happened?"

She said, "There was a man in the apartment all the time, hiding in the bedroom. I didn't know it until after you'd telephoned."

The freight car gave a series of quick jerks and bangs, slowed almost to a stop, then slammed in another string of cars, and after a moment the whole string began to roll.

"Sounds as though we're making up a train," I said. "Look here, do you suppose you could lie over on your side and I'd get over as close to you as I could? We'd lie back to back, and you could work on the knots on my wrists with your fingers, and I'd try to untie your wrists."

"We could try," she said.

We rolled and hitched along the floor until we were lying back to back. Somehow I couldn't get my fingers working. The cords around my wrists made my fumbling fingers seem all thumbs. But she was more successful. I felt the knot slip, heard her say, "I'm getting it, all right—ouch! I'll bet I lost a fingernail there—hold still, it's coming loose."

A few moments later my wrists were free. I sat up and untied her.

Abruptly, with that jerking lurch so characteristic of car switching, the engineer applied the brakes. Lorraine was thrown up against me, and I kept from falling only by grabbing at the side of the car. The partially opened door slammed back until it came up with a bang against the end of the iron track, leaving the square doorway wide-open. The whole string of cars abruptly slowed.

Suddenly our view was cut off. The doorway seemed to be pushed up against a solid wall of darkness.

"What is it?" Lorraine asked. "A warehouse?"

At that moment the train slammed to a dead stop.

I saw then that our car had been stopped directly opposite another string of boxcars.

"Can you jump across to the ladder on that car opposite?" I asked quickly.

She didn't even bother to answer, simply leaned out of the car. Caught the iron ladder on the car opposite, and stepped across. I had to wait a second for her to climb up, so as to leave me a handhold, and in that second the engine gave a snort and a jerk. The car started forward.

"Quick!" Lorraine shouted.

I just missed her leg as I grabbed an iron rung of the ladder and leaned out. It seemed that the car was literally jerked out from under me.

"You all right?" she asked.

"Yes, I took the shock on my other leg." I started down

107

the ladder. "Watch your step," I warned. "The—" I broke off, as I saw the flash of a red light, heard a little toot from the engine whistle, and saw the whole string of cars ahead slide to an abrupt stop. I saw the gleam of a flashlight, then another. Then a beam came slithering along the string of cars.

"Quick!" I said. "Get up to the top and lie down. They're searching for us."

I heard the slight scrape of her feet on the iron rungs as she scampered up the ladder, and I followed, making the best time I could. We flattened out, I on one side of the walk on top of the car, she on the other.

There were voices after that. Shadows danced along the side of a concrete warehouse just above us. I listened, trying to determine if these men were friends, sent by Gabby to rescue us, or if they were our captors returning. Then, within ten yards of me, a man's voice said, "This is the end of the cut. They must have swung off while it was moving. They're not in the car. You can see the ropes there on the floor. Why in hell can't Jim tie 'em so they stay tied!"

Another voice: "You can't hold things up any longer without making everybody suspicious. Give them the high-ball. We'll have to catch 'em as they leave the yards. We'll spread out. They can't get away."

Once more shadows danced. The switch engine gave two muted toots of the whistle and started the string of cars into rattling motion.

"Now what?" Lorraine asked.

"Now," I said, "we get out of here just as fast as we can. Come on, let's go."

"Where?"

"Back to the Redderstone Apartments. Unless I'm mistaken, we'll find a police inspector by the name of Fanston somewhere in the building, and we can get action out of him a whole lot quicker than we can explain to some strange cop. Tell me one thing. You said there was a man in your apartment?"

"Yes. He heard me talking on the telephone. I don't know whether you noticed it or not, but I gave an exclamation and then asked you to hold the line a minute."

"I noticed it," I said. "What happened?"

"A man stepped out of the bedroom. The first thing I knew I felt the cold circle of a gun muzzle sticking in the back of my neck. Then the man took me away from the telephone for a minute or two, and demanded to know who was talking. I told him it was just someone who wanted to return Muriel's purse."

"What did he do?" I asked.

"Marched me back to the telephone with instructions to get you up there at any cost and to insist that I was Muriel."

"And when I came up," I asked, "where was he?"

"In the bedroom. He had the door open a crack. He wasn't where he could see—only listen. That's why I took a chance and slipped out after you. All I wanted at the time was to get out. Later on, downstairs, when I saw the clerk on duty, I got the idea of trying to make you give up the purse. I was sure you had it under your coat."

"You knew that Muriel came to the hotel and got it back?"

"Yes, of course. She told me you gave it to her."

"Did she tell you what was in it?"

"No. What was in it?"

"Would you," I asked abruptly, "be shocked to learn Muriel is an enemy agent?"

"Good heavens! She can't be. Why, she's just a young married woman who found out she made a mistake and—"

"And what does she live on?"

"I don't know. She said she was looking for a job. I supposed she had some money—alimony, perhaps."

I didn't say anything for a few seconds, letting Lorraine get herself adjusted to the idea I'd given her. Then I said, "Just when did you meet Muriel?"

"A little over a week ago. She had an ad in the—"

"No, no. I mean tonight, after I left."

She said, "I pretended to go back up to the second floor to the apartment. That was just to fool you and the clerk. Actually, I just took the elevator all the way up to the top floor, waited for five or ten minutes, then went back down and walked out."

"The clerk was at the desk then?"

"No. No one was in the lobby."

"Where did you go?"

"There's a little tearoom down the block where Muriel usually drops in before she comes to the apartment to go to bed. I went there and waited, frightened stiff."

"How long did you wait?"

"It seemed like ages."

"But you don't know exactly how long it was?"

"No. It was quite a while."

"And she finally came in?"

"Oh, yes."

"That was before she had been to see us?"

"No, afterward. She had her purse."

"And you told her about what had happened in the apartment?"

"Yes."

"What did she do?"

"She seemed quite disturbed. She said she'd notify the police, but it would have to wait until tomorrow, because she had an important appointment to keep."

"And how did you happen to come down here to the switchyard?"

"I didn't want to go back to the apartment alone. Muriel said she had arranged for a pass and that I could come with her. She didn't seem particularly anxious to have me, though."

"Then you and Muriel came down here without first going back to the apartment?"

"That's right."

"Hadn't it occurred to you to call the police as soon as you got out of the apartment?"

"Of course."

"Why didn't you do it?"

"Because—well, Muriel's rather secretive about her affairs and somehow I had an idea she wouldn't like it. You see, she's had a divorce and—well, you know how those things are. I thought perhaps it might be something that was connected with the divorce, or an attempt on the part of her ex-husband to get evidence so he could get out of paying alimony, or something of that sort."

"Did Muriel tell you who she was meeting?"

"Yes, a man named Greester, but he never showed up."

"And what did he want?"

"Apparently it was something about her husband. Greester wasn't there, and Muriel didn't tell much. We started to walk down the tracks, and then the next thing I knew that car was almost on us. I think I screamed. I remember a man's arm around me, pulling me off the tracks; then I saw you and this other man jump off the car and start toward us. Then three men started toward you—there was that awful fight. I tried to help and—well, they grabbed me and tied me up."

"And Muriel?"

"Muriel got away."

"Anyone try to stop her?"

"I think one of the men did. He made a grab for her, but she jerked herself loose."

"It may have been an act?" I asked.

"It might have been an act," she said wearily.

I said, "All right, sister. Now I'm going to tell you something. Muriel is an enemy agent, and in case you want to know what was in that purse it was a great big wad of currency totaling seven thousand five hundred dollars. And *that's* why I was so cagey about delivering it."

Lorraine sat perfectly still on top of the boxcar, looking at me, her eyes wide and startled. After a while she said, "I can't believe it."

I didn't argue about it. I peered over the side of the car that was against the warehouse. "I think," I said, "we can manage to squeeze through here. We'll walk back down the length of the train, keeping behind these cars; and we'd better start. I'm going first."

It was dark as a pocket in the narrow space between the cars and the warehouse. There was just room to squeeze along, and I knew that if the train jerked into motion we'd be caught and rolled along between the moving cars and the warehouse until we dropped down under the wheels; but it was our only way out.

Halfway down the string of cars I crawled under and

looked back at the track. I could see little spots of light that stabbed the darkness, then they were snuffed out, only to glow again. They were still hunting for us.

"See anything?" Lorraine asked as I crawled back to the dark side of the cars.

"No," I said. There was no use scaring the kid to death.

We worked our way down to the end of the cars. There was a stretch of open track, curved rails running up to an iron bumper. Back of that was a concrete wall.

We were trapped.

I felt my way along the wall, hoping I might find a door. That was when Lorraine saw the flashlights.

"Look," she whispered. "*Lights!* I think they're coming this way."

I simply pulled her in behind the protection of that steel and concrete bumper.

We huddled there for what seemed five or ten minutes. The lights were coming closer. We could see shadows on the concrete wall.

The lights were swinging around now in wider arcs, making bright splotches on the concrete wall, intensifying the shadows. Then, when they must have been within twenty yards of us, they quit.

I got to my hands and knees, held my head low down, and peeked out. The track was a vague, distinct ribbon vanishing into a wall of darkness. I looked for several seconds and couldn't see anything. I decided to chance it.

We turned off the tracks when we came to the end of the warehouse, walked across the yards, and found a gate that was locked from the inside. We unlocked it and went out without seeing a soul.

"You have a key?" I asked Lorraine when we reached the Redderstone Apartments.

She opened her purse, fumbled around for a moment, and handed me a key.

I hesitated before putting it in the lock. "Someone on your floor have a dog?" I asked.

"Yes. I don't know which apartment it is. A cute little woolly dog."

"I heard him barking."

"Yes, he barks once in a while."

"Which end of the corridor from your apartment? Toward the front of the house or the back?"

"The back."

I fitted the key to the lock, held the door open, and Lorraine and I went in. The dimly lit foyer was silent as a tomb.

Halfway to the elevator I paused. "Look, Lorraine, you wait here. If you hear any commotion upstairs, get out just as fast as you can. Go to the nearest telephone and call police headquarters. If you *don't* hear anything, wait for me to come back and pick you up."

The door was locked with a night latch. I carefully inserted the key that Lorraine had given me and silently slipped back the latch. Then I eased the door open, ready to leap forward and go into action if necessary.

Gabby was sitting in the overstuffed chair, his feet propped up on a straight-backed chair, smoking a cigarette. He was all alone in the room.

"How," I asked, "did *you* get here?"

He turned and grinned. I saw, then, that his left eye was all puffed up. His lip had been cut, and when he grinned it opened up the cut and a few drops of blood started trickling down his chin.

I closed the door behind me. "How'd you make out?"

"Okay," Gabby said. "Did the Military find you?"

"No one found me. I rode a train out of the yards. What about the Military?"

Gabby said, "I sewed that place up. Nobody gets in or out, and they're going through it with a fine-tooth comb."

"Where," I asked, "did you get all that authority?"

"I didn't, I haven't, I ain't," Gabby said. "But in case I forgot to tell you I'm sort of working under a colonel here, and we're checking up on certain things that happened to freight shipments. At first we didn't think it could have heppened in the freight yards, because the records were all straight, but now we're changing our minds mighty fast. I came here to start tracing this stuff from the time it hit the terminal yards until it was delivered."

"Yes," I said, "you neglected to tell me."

Gabby grinned again. "I was afraid I had. Where's the girl spy?"

"That's what I wanted to ask you."

"Cripes!" Gabby said, frowning. "I thought you'd be able to keep *her* lined up."

"You mean you didn't see her?"

"No. What happened to her?"

"Just that she took to her heels is all I know."

Gabby straightened up. "Say, who do you think I'm talking about?"

"Muriel."

"Muriel nothing!" Gabby snorted. "Muriel's little roommate, Lorraine Dawson, is the one I mean."

"You're all wrong, but we won't argue that now. Where *is* Muriel?"

"In case it's any of your business," Gabby said angrily, "she's in the bedroom changing her clothes."

I started for the bedroom door.

Gabby said, "Don't."

"Why not?"

"She's a decent kid."

I said, "She may be a decent kid, but she's an enemy agent," and flung the door open.

Gabby came out of the chair and toward me fast, but something he saw in my face made him turn toward the bedroom.

It was empty.

"You see?"

Gabby walked across the room to the bedroom window and looked out to the iron platform of the fire escape.

After a minute I said, "Look, Gabby, we're going to get her back. She can't get away with it. I think Lorraine can help us."

Gabby turned. "Where is Lorraine?"

"Down by the elevator. I left her there while I came up to see that the coast was clear."

Gabby said, "Go get her. We can't wait."

Lorraine wasn't there.

I walked over to the door and looked out on the street.

She wasn't there. I came back and climbed the stairs. No sign of her on the stairs.

I went back to the apartment.

Gabby looked up. "Where is she?"

"I don't know," I said. "Suppose you and I quit making damned fools of ourselves. There was a dead man in that bedroom. I don't know what the big idea was with the police claiming it was a plant. You call the law in on a murder case and right away they start telling you it's all a pipe dream."

"I know," Gabby said.

"All right; it was a body. You can't pick up a body and carry it downstairs under your arm. You can't change the mattress and the sheet and the blankets and the spread and the pillows on a bed in the middle of the night. The way I see it, there's only one answer."

"The adjoining apartment?"

I nodded.

Gabby said, "How's your leg?"

"Okay."

Gabby said, "Remember, I've got my automatic, so in case the party gets rough let's not break any legs over it."

"We won't," I said.

Gabby said, "If you'd come down to earth and be reasonable—I could tell you what happened—just so you won't crack the wrong girl over the head."

"I won't crack the wrong girl."

"Look, Jay, when Muriel came to her apartment this evening she found a man's suit hanging in the closet. It looked as though the suit had just came back from the cleaners. She noticed a bulge in one pocket which turned out to be the seventy-five hundred."

"So little Muriel figures finders keepers."

"Muriel happens to be a gal who can look out for herself. The whole thing struck her as fishy, so she decided to sit tight until she discovered what was going on—or at least part of it. It seems there was quite a splash in the papers when her divorce came up and she's allergic to publicity. She had sense enough to realize that either by design or accident she had become involved in something, and she couldn't be sure her husband didn't have a hand in it. Unless it became absolutely necessary she didn't want the cops in on it."

"I still don't see why she carried all that around with her."

"She wanted to get it to a place of safekeeping, but a guy started to tail her when she left the apartment. She was almost sure she had lost him, but just as she was stepping out of the taxi she thought she saw him again. Apparently without Lorraine seeing her, she slipped her purse back on the seat and then got out. As soon as she was certain she had lost the tail she telephoned the cab company to see if the driver had found her purse."

"How come she didn't tell any of this to Lorraine?"

"I didn't ask her, but my guess is that she thought it would be best all around if she didn't."

"And the switch list with the message?"

"Don't be so damn sarcastic. A railroad friend of hers gave her that, earlier in the afternoon, and arranged for a pass. In case you want to know all about her private life, her husband made a property settlement prior to the divorce. Then he ran out on her and quit paying. This man tipped her off that a chap was working on the night shift at the hump who owed her husband a wad of dough, and told her that she could go down there tonight and he'd take her to this man. She wanted to get the rest of the money her husband had promised her on the property settlement and then forgot to pay."

"Who was this friend," I asked, "and will he corroborate her statement?"

I started for the window and got out onto the steel platform of the fire escape. The window which opened on the farther edge of the platform was closed. I slid my knife blade under it and found it wasn't locked.

"Step to one side as soon as you raise it," Gabby whispered.

I got the window up, and was too mad to care about anything. I slipped under Gabby's arm and went in headfirst. Gabby was behind me with the gun, and he could take care of anything that happened.

Nothing happened.

We were in an apartment very similar to the one we'd just left, only arranged in reverse order. The window opened into the bedroom. I could see the bed. It was clean and white, and apparently hadn't been slept in. For all I could see, there was no one in the apartment, and then somehow I had an uneasy feeling that the place was occupied. You could feel the presence of human beings.

We moved on a few steps from the window.

"The light switch will be over by the door," I whispered.

"Think we dare to risk the lights?" Gabby asked.

"Gosh, yes. This place gives me the willies."

"Stick 'em up!"

The beam of a flashlight sprang out of nothing and hit my eyes with such a bright glare that it hurt. I saw Gabby's wrist snap around so that his gun was pointed toward the flashlight. Then Inspector Fanston's voice yelled, "Hold it, soldier! This is the law."

Gabby said, "Put out that damn flashlight. What are you doing here?"

"What are *you* doing here?" the Inspector asked.

"There's no one here?" Gabby asked.

Fanston said, "Switch on the lights, Smitty."

The light switch clicked the room into illumination.

"Where's the girl?" I asked.

"What girl?" the Inspector asked.

"The one who came through the window a few minutes before we did."

"No one came through that window."

"For how long?"

"Ever since we came over here with you. I doped it out that if you saw a body it must have been moved. It looked as though it must have moved out the window to the fire escape, then across to here. I made a stall to get you boys out of the way, then Smitty and I went to work."

"And you've been waiting here all that time," I demanded, "simply on a hunch that the body might have been—"

"Take it easy," the Inspector interrupted. "Show him what we found, Smitty."

The cop opened the closet door.

I looked inside and saw a bundle of bedclothes wadded up into a ball. There were red splotches on the bedclothes—blood that wasn't old enough even yet to get that rusty-brown tint. It looked red and fresh.

"I'll be damned," Gabby said.

"That's the only way they could have come in," Fanston said. "It's perfectly logical. What's more, there are blood-stains on the iron ribs of the fire-escape platform."

"And why," I asked, "are you guarding the bloody bedclothes and letting the other apartment take care of it-self?"

Fanston looked at Smitty, and the look was a question.

"Why not?" Smitty said.

Fanston decided to tell us. "Because when we looked through that other apartment, we found something. I'll show you."

He led the way back through the window out to the fire escape and then to the girls' apartment. Over in a corner of the bedroom was a fine sprinkle of plaster dust on the floor near the baseboard.

Gabby was the one who got it first. He moved a mirror back out of the way. Behind it was a neat little hole in the plaster and the diaphragm of a dictograph.

The point established, we returned to the other apartment.

"The receiving end of the installation is in here," Fanston continued; "also, the bloody bedclothes are in here. You can figure what that means. Having put up that dictograph, with the receiving end in this apartment, they're naturally due to come back to watch it—if you fellows haven't messed things up so that you've scared away the quarry we're after."

Suddenly I remembered something. Without waiting to explain my hunch, I hurried out of the room.

I walked down the long corridor, looking at numbers on the doors. I found the apartment I wanted down at the far end of the peculiar clammy feel which clings to crowded apartment houses along toward morning. A dog yapped once, then quit.

I gently turned the doorknob. When I felt that the latch was free I pushed tentatively against the door.

The door was jerked open from the inside. Before I could let loose, I was thrown off balance and came stumbling on into the room.

A man's voice said, "All right—you asked for this."

It was dark in the room, with just the faint hint of distant lights seeping through the windows.

They had fed me enough carrots and vitamins to improve my night vision and taught me enough about rough-and-tumble fighting in the dark, so that what came next didn't bother me at all. It was just like going through a training routine.

I knew a blackjack was swinging for my head somewhere in the darkness. I sidestepped, felt a swish of air as something whizzed past where my head had been, saw a dark object in front of me, and, somewhat off balance, figured out where his bread basket would be, and hit him where he was thickest.

I felt surprised muscles collapsing beneath the force of my blow, heard a *whoosh* as the breath went out of him.

Someone cursed behind me. A flame split the darkness wide open. I could feel the hot breath of burning gunpowder against my cheek. I never did hear the bullet crash. My ears were numbed by the sound, but I whirled and struck out with my left.

It was then the knee gave way. I went down in a heap. But they'd taught me all about that in the Army too. I caught the man's knees as I went down. He struck at my head in the dark with the gun barrel and missed by a couple of inches. I grabbed for his wrists and didn't connect. He kicked me in the shin and broke loose.

There was a quarter second of silence. I realized then he had enough light to show him where I was. He was going to shoot.

I flung myself into a quick roll, kicking as I came over. My heel grazed against his knee. A dog was barking frenziedly.

I heard running steps in the corridor. The beam of a flashlight danced around the opening of the door. There were scrambling steps, someone barking an order, a back door opening, and a pell-mell of stampeding feet running down a staircase.

The two officers went storming past me, following the beam of the flashlight. I saw Gabby's long arms raise the window, saw him slide matter-of-factly out to the edge of the sill, and heard him say, "All right, boys. That'll be enough. Stick up your hands."

The windowpane above him split into fragments of glass as two bullets crashed through.

I saw Gabby's arm swing the automatic.

"You all right, Jay?" he asked.

I rolled over on my hands and knees and started getting up. The knee felt weak, the way a thumb feels when you've bent it all the way back and all the strength is gone out of it; but I could hobble along all right.

"Okay," I said.

I went into the bedroom. Before I found the light switch, I could see two long rolls of something stretched out on the bed. Then I found the switch and clicked on illumination.

They were tied up in sheets, their lips taped shut. Two pair of eyes looked up at me—large expressive dark eyes and big blue eyes.

I reached over and tried pulling off the tape from their lips. I held the side of Lorraine's cheek, got a good hold on the tape, and gave it a quick jerk.

"Hurt?" I asked.

She looked up at me. "Not much."

I went around the bed to Muriel, worked a corner loose, and then gave her the same treatment.

"You *would* have to do it the hard way!" she flared.

I started untying sheets.

From the outer room I heard Inspector Fanston saying in an odd voice, "Good Lord! How did you do it, shooting in the dark? Knocking the legs out from under them."

Gabby didn't even bother to answer the question. He said, "Listen, Inspector, this is purely civilian, see? We don't figure in it at all. We're just witnesses who happened to be in an apartment in the building. Here's a number. Call this number and make a report. They'll tell you what to do.

As far as you know, it's a gang of housebreakers that had headquarters here. You even keep the railroad angle out of it. Get me?"

I waited, expecting to hear Fanston ask Gabby who the hell he thought he was. But, instead, Fanston's voice sounded meek and subdued. I knew then the shield in the leather case Gabby was carrying in his pocket was big stuff.

The Inspector said, "I get you. Smitty, go out in the hallway and get those people back where they belong. Tell them there may be more shooting. And don't let anyone talk with the prisoners."

I heard the whir of a telephone and Inspector Fanston's voice saying "Police Headquarters," then Muriel Comley saying, "Leave that sheet where it is. All I've got on is underwear." Her eyes went past me to the doorway and softened. "Oh, hello, Gabby!"

Gabby said, "We can stay right here until things quiet down, and then you can go and—"

"Not in *this* room," Lorraine said.

"What's the matter with it?" Gabby asked.

I looked at Lorraine's eyes, got up and walked across to the closet door, opened it a few inches, and then hastily pushed it shut.

Gabby took one look at my face and knew the answer.

"Oh, Fanston," he said, "the body you're looking for is in here."

Over a breakfast of ham, eggs, and coffee, Gabby told us as much as he ever told us.

"For a long time," he said, "we'd been running into a peculiar type of trouble. Machinery would be tested and double-tested. It would be put aboard freight cars, shipped to various Army camps, and tested when it got there. Everything would be all right, but after a while, usually under the stress of combat, the machinery would suddenly go haywire. Part of it we found was due to the old familiar sabotage of putting a little acid on critical metal parts, and then carefully covering up the slight discoloration.

"But the other part of it had us completely baffled. A

machine would get into combat and suddenly fail. Later on, we'd post-mortem, and find sugar had been introduced into the gasoline. You know what *that* does to an internal combustion motor.

"After a while we found out that all the machinery with which we had this trouble had come through the yards in this city, but that in itself didn't seem to mean anything, because the machinery was tested on arrival at destination and everything was seemingly all right. But we still kept coming back to the peculiar coincidence that our troubles came only with stuff that went through these freight yards.

"I'd had some railroad experience, and I was sent up here to check the whole situation. In the meantime, Carl Greester was working on the hump, and he stumbled onto what was going on. The enemy agents had duplicate tags slightly larger than the regular numbered tags which went on the cars as they came through the switch. By putting on those phony numbers they'd have the cars they wanted switched down to a siding where they had sufficient opportunity to do their work. And it didn't take them long.

"After the cars had been entered and sabotaged they'd be resealed, the phony numbers taken off, a couple of dummy cars added, and a switch engine sent down to pick up the cut and redistribute it.

"When Greester found out what was happening, he didn't go to the F.B.I. He went to the men who were mixed up in it. They bought his silence for seven thousand five hundred dollars. But Greester was afraid to take a bribe in the ordinary manner, and they weren't foolish enough to just park seven thousand five hundred somewhere and go away and leave it for him to pick up. Greester kept insisting that the money be given to him under such circumstances that if there was a double-cross, the F.B.I. couldn't claim he had accepted a bribe.

"Finally they agreed that Greester would send a suit out to be cleaned. When the suit came back, it was to be given to the clerk to hang up in Greester's apartment. The bribe money would be in the inside pocket. In that way, if anyone suspected what was happening, Greester could have a perfect alibi. He'd sent his suit to the cleaners. The cleaner had returned the suit to the clerk while Greester was at the yards.

"But when the go-between picked up the suit at the cleaners, planted the seventy-five hundred bucks in the pocket, and handed the suit to the desk, he either got mixed up on the numbers, or the clerk did. No names were mentioned, merely apartment numbers. The suit went to two-eighteen instead of two-eight-one.

"Greester came home, looked for the suit and the bribe money. No suit, no money. He asked the clerk if anything had been left for him at the desk. The clerk said no. The gang knew the suit had been delivered. They thought the clerk had got the dough.

"They got the thing straightened out, finally. The clerk was a little nincompoop who was always getting figures mixed up. They decided he must have delivered the suit to the wrong apartment. One of the men got into Muriel's apartment with a passkey and found the suit; but the money was gone. He was in there when Lorraine came in, and he had an idea the money might have found its way into Muriel's purse. That's why he was so interested in the telephone conversation."

"And the clerk?" I asked.

"The clerk kept thinking over Greester's questions, finally remembered about the suit, and wondered if he hadn't put it in two-eighteen instead of two-eighty-one. He went up to two-eighteen, let himself in with a passkey, and found a man boring holes in the wall and installing a dictograph. We know what happened to the clerk."

"Why the dictograph?" I asked.

"Don't you see? They didn't know whether Muriel was a government agent and they were leading with their chins, or whether it was just a mixup. Naturally, killing the clerk hadn't entered into their plans. They had to get rid of the body."

"They knew we'd discovered that body?" I asked.

"Sure they did. They were on the other end of the dictograph when we stumbled on it before they'd had a chance to remove it. They evidently waited a while to see if we were going to report it. When they found out we didn't, they tried to whisk it away."

"But Greester must have thrown in with them," I said. "His apartment was two-eight-one—"

"He didn't throw in with them," Gabby said. "Greester tried to play smart. It was unfortunate that he did."

"You mean—?"

"The police discovered his body about daylight this morning, when one of the gang confessed."

"But," Muriel said, "Carl Greester seemed so nice. He told me that a man who owed my husband some money was working down at the switchyard on a night shift, that if I'd come down and see him I could arrange to get the balance of the money that was due under the property settlement with my husband. He wrote out where I was to meet him shortly after midnight. I . . . Oh, I guess I see now."

Gabby said, "He found out about this man and tipped you off just as a favor, but all the time he was playing with this personal dynamite. He thought he was being smart. He was signing his own death warrant."

"So they took over Greester's apartment?" I asked.

"Sure. It was bad enough finding Greester's suit in the girls' apartment. But when the girls came down to the switchyard to join Greester around midnight, they became suspicious. They made an excuse to grab Muriel, jerk her out of the way of a freight car, and frisk her purse while they were doing it. As soon as they found out that the purse contained seventy-five hundred dollars, the girls were on the spot. Then you and I put in our two-bits' worth."

"What's become of the money?" I asked.

"The money," Gabby said, "is in the hands of Uncle Sam. Three men were placed under arrest for tampering with the seals of freight cars. One of them started talking. He's talked enough so Fanston can pin the murder of the clerk and Carl Greester on the two other men. And the third, who turned state's evidence, will get life as an accessory after the fact."

"How about the man who owed my husband money?" Muriel asked. "Is he one of them?"

Gabby shook his head. "I think you're okay on that. His name is Gulliver. He works under Bob Cuttering, Cuttering's a grouchface who is pretty much overworked, but he's a good egg just the same."

I said, "I don't see why this man in the bedroom didn't stick me up for Muriel's purse—"

"Because you *said* you didn't have it with you. Lorraine could tell, from the way you were holding your left arm against your body, that you did have it. The man in the bedroom could only hear what you'd said. He couldn't see. That's why Lorraine was able to get out of the apartment—talking as though she were slamming the door indignantly on her visitor, but actually slamming herself on the other side of it."

Lorraine said, "I was never so frightened in my life. While I was waiting down there, a man poked the muzzle of a gun into my back and marched me down the corridor."

"The dog was a sort of watchman?" I asked.

Gabby nodded. "When they moved into Greester's apartment they took the dog with 'em. The dog had been trained on one of those inaudible dog whistles. Whenever he heard it he'd bark and try to get out. Whenever anyone entered the place who might make trouble, a guy posted outside would blow the whistle, and the dog would bark. The dog had also been taught to give warning when anyone came near the apartment."

"Well," I said, "I guess that winds up the case."

"Of course," Gabby said, "the colonel insists that he's going to hold us responsible to see nothing happens to these girls—my buddy and me. I told the colonel it might be a little embarrassing. But you know the colonel; he just barked into the telephone, 'Keep those two girls lined up, I don't want them going out with anyone except you and Jay!'"

"You mean we can't have any dates," Muriel demanded, "unless—"

"Exactly," Gabby said sternly. "Those are orders direct from the colonel."

Muriel lowered her lashes. "Well," she conceded, "if it's for my country."

I looked at Lorraine.

She said, "He's got the idea now, Gabby, so you can take your foot away. It's *my* toe you're on."

"What are you two talking about?" Muriel demanded.

"Our patriotic duty to our government," Lorraine said self-righteously.

PEGGY CASTLE and UNCLE BENEDICT in

THE JEWELED BUTTERFLY

There was an office rumor that Old E.B. locked the door of his private office on Wednesday mornings so he could practice putting. This had never been confirmed, but veteran employees at the Warranty Exchange & Fidelity Indemnity, known locally as WEFI, made it a rule either to take up important matters on Tuesday or to postpone them until Thursday.

Peggy Castle, E.B.'s secretary, didn't inherit the Wednesday breathing spell from her predecessors. When Old E.B. found out that before coming to WEFI, Peggy had worked on a country newspaper upstate he inveigled her into starting a gossip column in the WEFI house organ.

Peggy was interested in people, had a photographic memory for names and faces, and a broadminded, whimsical sense of humor. The result was that her column, which she called *Castle's in the Air*, attracted so much attention that Old E.B., beaming with pride, insisted she devote more and more time to it.

"It's just what we've needed," he said. "We've had too much money to spend on the damn paper. We made it too slick, too formal, too dressed up. It looked impressive, but who the hell wants a house organ to be impressive? We want it to be neighborly. We want it to be interesting. We want the employees to eat it up. We want something that'll attract customer attention on the outside. You're doing it. It's fine. Keep it up. One of these days it'll lead to something big."

Old E.B. carried a bunch of clippings from Peggy's column in his wallet. Very often he'd pick out priceless gems and sidle up to cronies at the club. "Got a girl up at the office—my secretary, smart as a whip," he'd begin. "You ought to see what she's done to the gossip column in our house organ. This is it. *Castle's in the Air.* Listen to this one:

" 'The identity of the practical joker in the Bond Writing Department has not as yet been discovered. When Bill Fillmore finds him he insists he's going to choke him until his eyeballs protrude far enough to be tattooed with Bill's initials. It seems that Bill and Ernestine have been keeping pretty steady company. At noon on last Thursday, Bill decided to pop the question, did so, and was accepted. That afternoon he was walking on air. However, it seems that Bill had confided his intentions to a few friends, showing them the ring he had bought to slip on Ernestine's finger if she said yes. So some wag managed to dust the knees of Bill's trousers immediately after lunch. Bill doesn't know how it was done. He didn't even know it had been done. While Ernestine was telling the news and showing her sparkler, observant eyes were naturally looking Bill over. People couldn't refrain from seeing the two well-defined dust spots on the knees of Bill's trousers. Ernestine thought it was cute, but Bill—well, let's talk about something else.'

"How's that for a yarn?" E.B. would say, slapping his crony on the back. "Damnedest thing you ever heard? You can figure what that's done to the house organ. Everybody reads it now. Stuff like that really peps it up.

"How's that? Hell, no! Not a word of truth to it, but the funny thing is that Bill Fillmore doesn't know it. He really thinks there *was* dust on his trousers, put there by some wag, and he's going around chewing tenpenny nails. Half of the people in the place are in on the secret, and the other half are looking for the practical joker. Damnedest thing you ever saw, the way stuff like that peps up the house organ. Here's more of it."

Given the slightest provocation, Old E.B. would pull out more clippings. Usually his cronies gave him the provocation. The clippings were always good for a laugh, and many of E.B.'s friends had house-organ problems of their own.

On this Wednesday afternoon, Peggy opened the anonymous letter and read it through carefully.

Don Kimberly is having a date tonight at the Royal Pheasant with Miss Cleavage. Is this going to burn somebody up! I don't ask you to take my word for it, so I won't sign my name. Just stick around and see what happens.

The missive was signed *A Reader,* and the writing was feminine.

Ordinarily she would have consigned this sort of thing to the wastebasket after only a cursory glance, but Don Kimberly, troubleshooter in the Claims Adjusting Department, was the most eligible catch in the organization. A young, clear-headed bachelor with a legal education, he had dark wavy hair, steady slate-colored eyes, bronzed skin, and a rather mysterious air of reserve. Every girl in the organization got cardiac symptoms when he walked by her desk—and Peggy was no exception.

"Miss Cleavage" was Stella Lynn, who had won a beauty contest at a country fair before coming to the city to work for WEFI. It was obvious that the judges of this local show had been more interested in well-developed curves than in streamlined contours.

Stella Lynn, proud of her curvaceousness, habitually wore the most plunging necklines of any employee in the WEFI organization. When someone came up with the nickname of "Miss Cleavage," the appellation had fit as snugly as the office dresses she wore and had stuck like chewing gum.

Peggy Castle studied the anonymous letter again.

What in the world could Don Kimberly see in Stella Lynn? The whole thing was ridiculous enough, so that it *could* have been a gag sent to her by some practical joker who hoped she would publish it in her column without confirmation and so create a minor office furor.

On the other hand, suppose the thing actually was true? It would cause plenty of commotion.

Without stopping to think that this was exactly what the writer of the anonymous letter had planned, Peggy decided to find out at first-hand. . . .

The Royal Pheasant night club catered to a regular clientele. The floor show was spotty, the food quite good, the music fair. The dance floor was a little larger than the handkerchief-sized squares in some of the more expensive night clubs.

Peggy, using her press card to forestall any rule about unescorted women guests, sallied into the Royal Pheasant attired in her best semi-formal, secured a table, and toyed with a cocktail, waiting.

Half an hour passed uneventfully. The headwaiter dropped by. "Another cocktail, Miss Castle?"

She started slightly at his use of her name and then, remembering the press card, smiled and shook her head.

"We want you to be happy," the headwaiter went on, "and we hope you will write something nice about the place."

Peggy felt a twinge of conscience. Perhaps the management thought she was with some magazine of large circulation.

"As a matter of fact," he went on, "I read your column every single issue."

"*You* do?" she asked, surprised.

"E.B. Halsey told me about your column," the headwaiter went on. "He comes in her quite often. He put me on the mailing list. It's very good stuff."

Peggy felt a surge of relief. "Oh. I'm so glad—so glad you like it."

"We get quite a bit of business from the big brass out at your company," he went on. "We're really pleased that you're here. And of course, you'll be entitled to all the courtesies."

"All the courtesies?" she repeated.

"The tab is on the house," he explained. "Another cocktail?"

"No, thanks, not right now."

"We have a good show tonight. Glad you're here."

He moved away, taking with him a load of guilt from Peggy's shoulders and leaving her with a queer feeling of exultation.

Then Don Kimberly came in—alone.

Quite evidently he had a table reserved. He seated himself, looked leisurely around, ordered a cocktail and settled back with the air of a man who has arrived early for an appointment.

Peggy glanced at her wrist watch. It was 9:15. The floor show started at 9:30.

Peggy puckered her forehead. It was bizarre enough in the first place to think of Don Kimberly taking Stella Lynn to the Royal Pheasant. But he certainly wasn't expecting Miss Cleavage to come in unescorted and join him. There was something strange about the whole business. If it had been a date he'd have called for Stella and escorted her.

Peggy became so immersed in her thoughts that she didn't realize the passing of time until the lights dimmed and her waiter was there with another cocktail.

"Beg pardon, Miss Castle, but the management knows another one won't hurt you, and you'll be wanting to watch the floor show now."

Peggy thanked him. The chorus came dancing on, undraped almost to the point of illegality. A master of ceremonies pulled up the microphone.

Peggy glanced at Don Kimberly. Kimberly wasn't watching the girls' legs. He was frowningly contemplating his wrist watch.

Good heavens, Peggy Castle thought, she wouldn't stand him up. She wouldn't *dare*. Why, this is the highlight of her career. If she actually has a date with him she—no, no, she couldn't be late.

But quite obviously, whoever Don Kimberly was waiting for *was* late, and the increasing shortness of the intervals at which he consulted his watch and then gave frowning attention to the door indicated a rapidly growing impatience.

And then the lights came on, and suddenly Peggy realized that Don Kimberly was looking at her with the puzzled expression of "where-the-devil-have-I-seen-that-girl-before" in his eyes.

She nodded and smiled, and as he bowed she saw sudden recognition flash in his face. Then he was on his way over.

"Well, hello, Miss Castle," he said. "I didn't recognize you for a moment. Waiting for someone?"

"Oh, no," she said. "I'm getting material for my column, covering a nitery where so many of the WEFI officials drop in. I trust you realize that the eyes of the press are upon you, Mr. Kimberly, and that the pitiless white light of publicity will be turned on you in my next—"

"Oh, good heavens!" Kimberly exclaimed in dismay, and, without asking her permission, sat down at her table and scowled at her.

"Why, what's the matter?" Peggy asked vivaciously. "Surely *you* have nothing to conceal. You're unmarried, unencumbered. I—was on the point of adding uninhibited."

"Uninhibited is right," he groaned.

"And may I ask why being written up in *Castle's in the Air* seems to provoke so little enthusiasm in you?"

"Am I unenthusiastic?"

"I thought you were."

He smiled, quite evidently having regained his composure. "I'm enthusiastic now, but it's certainly not because of your column."

"Surely *you* aren't alone?" she asked archly, carefully surveying his face.

"I'm waiting for some folks. Why not quit playing with that cocktail and let me order you another?"

"Good heavens, this is my second."

"Well, at the rate you're working on that one, the first must have been at least an hour ago. Here, waiter!"

Peggy let him have his way. She was experiencing a pleasant glow, not only from the drinks, but from the exciting realization that there must be more to this than appeared on the surface.

Why had Don Kimberly made this surreptitious rendezvous with Stella Lynn? Had he been ashamed to go to her apartment and escort her to the Royal Pheasant—or had he been afraid to?

Once more Kimberly glanced at his wrist watch.

"My, you're jittery," Peggy said. "Like a nervous cat. You aren't by any chance being stood up, are you? No, that's catty! After all, you know, I'm on the lookout for news."

She felt certain he winced inwardly. "A news story," he said, "has been defined as being the thing the other person doesn't want published. I believe there was some famous newspaperman who said, 'If the parties want it published, it's not news. If they try to keep it out of the paper, then it's news.'"

"And are you going to try to keep something out of the paper?" she asked.

Abruptly he was serious. "Yes, I'm afraid I'm going to deprive you of a choice item for your column—even if I have to go direct to E. B. Halsey to do it."

"The date you have here tonight?"

He regarded her with frowning appraisal. "Now, wait a minute, Miss Castle. Why are *you* here?"

She met his eyes. "I received an anonymous tip that you and Stella Lynn were going to be here tonight. I thought I'd drop in, cover the night club, and pick up a 'personal' that would be—well, interesting—to a lot of people at the office."

"You mean amusing?"

"Well, if we're going to be technical about it, amusement is a form of interest."

Kimberly was thoughtful. "You've doubtless heard the nickname 'Miss Cleavage'," he said at length.

Peggy started to laugh, and then at something in his tone caught herself.

"I've known her for five years," Kimberly went on, "I knew her before she came to work here, knew her before she won that beauty contest. She's a good kid."

"I'm sorry," Peggy said. "I—"

"You don't need to be. I understand. She—I don't know, I guess she's an exhibitionist. She has that complex. Just as some people like to sing, Stella likes to show her curves. She's proud of them. But she's a good kid."

Peggy said, "I didn't realize that there was anything

serious—"

"There isn't."

"I know, but what I'm trying to say is that I don't think there's anyone in the company who realizes that you've known her so long. You are, of course—well, eligible. I guess everybody likes Stella, but people wouldn't expect you two to be having a date."

Abruptly he said, "I like her, but this isn't a date, and I'm worried."

"What do you mean?"

He said, "As you probably know, my job is pretty diversified. If an actress reports she's lost fifty thousand dollars' worth of jewels, or claims that someone got into her apartment and stole a hundred-thousand-dollar necklace, it's up to me to investigate. I handle the burglary-insurance division of WEFI, and that ties in with a lot of things."

She nodded, her senses alert.

"Stella called me on the telephone this morning. To appreciate the significance of that you must realize that Stella has always had an exaggerated idea of the importance of my position. This is, I think, the first time she ever called me, and she called me during office hours."

Kimberly paused and glanced searchingly at her. Peggy kept her face expressionless.

"Well," he went on, "she told me that she had to see me tonight on a terribly important matter. She asked me where we could meet. I said I'd be glad to see her at any time or place, and she said it must be someplace where the meeting would seem to be accidental. So I suggested the Royal Pheasant. She said this would be all right, and that she'd be here at nine thirty on the dot."

"She was to meet you here?"

"Yes. I offered to call for her at her apartment. She said I mustn't go near her place, that she was in a ticklish situation, and that I should meet her here. If she was with someone I was to pretend it was an accidental meeting. She promised to be here by nine thirty sharp. I'm worried."

"I didn't know, and I guess no one else did, that you were friends."

"There's no particular secret about it. Stella thought it would be better if we didn't proclaim it from the housetops. You see, she may be an exhibitionist, but she has a delicately adjusted sense of values, and she'll never let a friend down. She's a good kid. She's oversensitive about the difference in our positions at the place."

"I take it you got her the job?"

"No, I didn't. I don't know who did. I ran into her in the elevator one afternoon. She told me she had been working there for two weeks. I offered to buy her a drink. She told me she realized I was up in the high brass and she was only in the filing department. She said she wanted me to know she'd never embarrass me.

"It's things like that about Stella that make you like her. She's so natural, always so perfectly frank and easy. Look here, Miss Castle, I'm worried about her. I'm going up to her apartment and make sure she's all right. It might be a good thing if you came along."

"Perhaps she's just late and—"

"Not Stella. She'd have phoned if she'd been detained. Waiter, let's have a check, please."

Peggy didn't tell him she had had no dinner. She merely nodded and gave him a smile she hoped was reassuring. "I'll be glad to go with you," she said, "but I thought Stella told you that you mustn't go to her apartment."

"That's right, but I think that with you with me it'll be all right. We'll say you and I had a date for tonight—that we're together. And anything you may find out isn't for publication. Come on, let's go."

The apartment house was ornate in front, but rather shabby after one had passed the foyer. Almost mechanically Don Kimberly fitted a key to the front door, opened it, escorted Peggy through the foyer, back to the automatic elevator, and punched the button for the fifth floor.

"You have—a key?" she asked.

"Don't be silly. That's the key to my own apartment house. Almost any key will fit these outer doors."

Peggy knew that was so, knew also that Don Kimberly hadn't so much as hesitated or tentatively tried his key. He had fitted it to the lock, turned it with complete assurance, and gone in without pausing.

She found herself wondering whether this was the first time he had tried his own key in that lock. The fact that she hated herself for having the thought didn't erase it from her mind.

Then the rattling elevator came to a stop. Kimberly held the door open for her and slid the steel door of the elevator shut behind him. "Down to your left," he said. "Five nineteen."

She turned left, and Kimberly, catching up with her, pushed the bell button of Apartment 519.

They could hear the sound of the buzzer, but no sound of motion.

Kimberly waited a few moments, then tried the door. The knob turned, the door opened, and Peggy, looking in, saw a well-ordered, plainly furnished apartment.

"Anybody home?" Kimberly called.

Peggy clutched his arm.

"What is it?" he asked.

"That coat over the chair."

"What about it?"

"It's a coat she'd have worn going out for the evening. Why would she have left it here?"

She pointed to a swinging door that evidently led to a kitchen. Her voice sounded high-pitched with excitement. "Let's make sure she isn't here."

Kimberly pushed back the swinging door. Peggy, who was standing where she could see through the half-open door, gave an exclamation.

The stockinged legs of a girl were sprawled out on the floor. A bottle of whiskey was on the side of the sink. A glass had rolled from the girl's limp fingers, leaving a trail of liquid along the linoleum. The figure was attired in a strapless bra, a voluminous petticoat, shoes, and stockings.

Kimberly suddenly laughed and called, "Stella, come on, wake up! You've missed the boat!"

The woman didn't move.

Peggy, moving forward, noticed the peculiar color of the girl's skin. She dropped swiftly to her knees, picked up the limp hand, and suddenly dropped it. "She's dead."

"What!"

"Dead. It must have been her heart."

Kimberly said, "Call a doctor."

Peggy said, "A doctor won't help. She's dead. Just touch her, and you'll know she's dead. We'd better—"

"Better what?"

"Better call the police."

Kimberly hesitated. "What's that on her leg?"

Peggy looked at the girl's right leg. Attached to the reinforced top of the sheer nylon stocking was a beautiful butterfly pin with diamonds, rubies, and emeralds giving a splash of glittering color.

"Good heavens," Kimberly exclaimed, "how in the world did she get *that*?"

"Why, what about it?" Peggy asked, realizing that Kimberly's face had turned white.

"Ever hear of the Garrison jewel theft?" he asked.

"Who hasn't?"

"Our company insured the Garrison jewels. We're stuck to the tune of two hundred and fifty thousand dollars—and that butterfly looks exactly like the famous Garrison butterfly. Now, how in the world did Stella get that?"

Peggy unfastened the butterfly pin and dropped it into her purse. "It won't do any good to have the police find that," she said.

"Look here," Kimberly protested. "You can't do that. It may be evidence."

"Of what?"

"I don't know. I only know you can't do that."

"I've already done it."

"But—look here, let's call a doctor and—we don't need to wait. Let the doctor do whatever's necessary."

Peggy said, "It's a job for the police. Do you notice that froth on her lips? And there's an odor that I have been trying to place. Now I know what it is."

"What do you mean, an odor?"

"Bitter almonds. That means cyanide. So does the color of the skin."

He looked at her dubiously. "You seem to know a lot about—suicides."

"I do," Peggy said. "I've done newspaper work. Now, since we're already in it this deep, let's take a look around."

"What for?"

"To protect ourselves. Let's make certain there are no more corpses, for one thing."

She moved swiftly about the apartment, her quick eyes drinking in details.

"If this is suicide, what you're doing is probably highly illegal," he said.

"And if it's murder?"

"Then it's doubly illegal."

She said nothing, moving quietly around the rooms. Her gloved hands occasionally touched some object with the greatest care, but for the most part her hands were at her sides.

There was an odor of raw whiskey about the place, perhaps from the spilled drink in the kitchen. However, the odor was stronger in the bathroom.

Peggy dropped to her knees on the tiled floor, picked up a small sliver of glass, then another. She let both slivers drop back to the tiles.

In the bedroom, the dress Stella was to have worn was spread out on the bed. The plunging neckline seemed to go nearly to the waist.

Kimberly, looking at the V-shaped opening in the front of the dress, gave a low whistle. "Peggy," he said at length, using her first name easily and naturally, "this is going to make a stink. If it should be murder—I don't see how it could be, and yet that's what I'm afraid of."

"Suppose it's suicide?" she asked.

"Then there wouldn't be too much to it—just a few lines on page two, or perhaps a write-up in the second section. And Old E. B. hates bad publicity."

"Are you telling me?"

"Well, then," he said, "do you think we really have to notify the police? Can't we just call a doctor and leave?"

"Do you want to be Suspect Number One in a murder case?" she asked.

"Heavens, no!"

"You're filing nomination papers right now with that sort of talk. There's the phone. Call the police."

He hesitated. "I'd like to keep us out of it altogether. Since she's dead there's nothing we can do—"

Peggy walked to the phone, dialed the operator, asked for police headquarters, and almost immediately heard a booming masculine voice answer the phone.

Peggy said, "My name is Castle. I wish to report a death. We just found a body under very odd circumstances and—"

"Where are you?"

Peggy gave the address.

"Wait there," the voice said. "Don't touch anything. Be on the lookout for a squad car. I'll get in touch with the dispatcher."

The two officers were very considerate. They listened to the sketchy story Kimberly told, the story that very carefully left out all reference to Peggy's suspicion of poison, and recounted barely the facts that Stella Lynn was a "friend of theirs," that they had called on her at her apartment, had found the door open, walked in, and discovered her body on the floor; they didn't know exactly what the proper procedure was under the circumstances, but felt they should notify the police.

The police looked around a bit, nodded sagely, and then one of them called the coroner.

Peggy ventured with some hesitation, "Are you—have you any ideas of what caused death?"

"You thinking of suicide?"

She hesitated, "I can't help wondering whether it might have been her heart."

"Had she been despondent or anything?"

"I didn't know her that well," Peggy said, "but I gather she had rather a happy disposition. But—well, notice the foam on the lips, the peculiar color of her skin—"

The officer shrugged. "We aren't thinking, not right now. We're following rules and taking statements."

There followed an interval of waiting. Men came and went, and eventually the Homicide Squad arrived with a photographer to take pictures of the body, and a detective to question Peggy and Kimberly in detail.

138

Kimberly told his story first. Since it did not occur to anyone to examine them separately, Peggy, after hearing Don's highly generalized version of the evening's activities, confined herself to the bare essentials. The officer seemed to take it for granted that she had been Don Kimberly's date, and that following dinner they had dropped in at Stella Lynn's apartment simply because they were friends and because Stella Lynn worked in the same office.

Don Kimberly drove her home. Peggy hoped he would open up with some additional explanation, but he was completely preoccupied with his thoughts and the problem of driving through the evening traffic, so it became necessary for Peggy to bring up the subject.

"You told your story first," she said, "so I had to back your play, but I think we've carried it far enough."

"What do you mean?"

"The police assumed I was your date for the evening."

"Well, what's wrong with that? We can't help what they assume."

"Then I'll draw you a diagram," Peggy said impatiently. "I think Stella Lynn was murdered. I think it was carefully planned, cold-blooded, deliberate murder, cunningly conceived and ruthlessly carried out. I think the police are going to investigate enough to find that out. Then they're going to ask *you* to tell *your* story in greater detail."

He slowed the car until it was barely crawling. "All right," he said, "what's wrong with my story? You and I were at the Royal Pheasant. We got to talking about Stella Lynn. We decided to run over and see her. We—"

"Everything is wrong with that story," she interrupted. "In the first place, someone knew you were going to the Royal Pheasant to meet Stella. That someone sent me an anonymous letter. Moreover, if the police check with the headwaiter, they'll learn that I came in alone, using my press card, and that you came in later."

Abruptly he swung the car to the curb and shut off the motor.

"What time did you get that anonymous letter?"

"In the afternoon mail."

"What became of it?"

"I tore it into small bits and dumped it into the wastebasket."

He said, "Stella didn't work today. She rang up and told the personnel manager she wouldn't be at the office. About ten thirty she rang me up and asked me what our policy would be on paying out a reward for the recovery of all the gems in the Garrison job."

"What did you tell her?"

"I told her it made a great deal of difference with whom we were dealing. You know how those things are. It's our policy never to reward a thief. If we did, we'd be in the position of fencing property that had first been stolen from our own clients. But if a man gives us a legitimate tip and that tip leads to the recovery of insured property, we are, of course, willing to pay, and pay generously."

"You told her that?"

"Yes."

"What did she say?"

"She told me she thought she had some information on the Garrison case that would interest me. I told her that on a big job like that hundreds of false leads were floating around. She told me that she could show me evidence that would prove she was dealing with people who knew what they were talking about."

"That," Peggy said, "would account for the jeweled butterfly."

"You mean that was to be my assurance I was dealing with the right people?"

"That was the start of it, but I think it has an added significance now."

"What?"

"You are thinking Stella ran into danger because she was going to tell you something about the Garrison jewels. Now, let's suppose you are right, and she was killed by the jewel thieves. They'd never have left that jeweled butterfly on her stocking. All those rubies, emeralds, and diamonds! It must be worth a small fortune."

He thought that over.

"And," Peggy went on, "if she'd been killed by an intruder or a burglar he'd naturally have taken the butterfly.

So it adds up to the fact that her death must have been un- related to that Garrison job and must have been caused by someone who was so anxious to have her out of the way the opportunity to steal the butterfly meant nothing."

He looked at her with sudden respect. "Say, you're a log- ical little cuss."

She said, "That's not what women want. When men praise their brains it's almost a slam. A woman would far rather be known as a glamor puss than as a thinker. Let's check on our story a little further. Stella telephoned you this morning, and it was you who suggested the Royal Pheasant?"

"That's right. Surely *you* don't doubt my statement."

"I don't doubt your statement. I doubt your conclusions."

"What do you mean?"

"If you told me that two and three added up to ten," she said, "I wouldn't be doubting your statement, I'd be doubt- ing your conclusions. You might actually have ten as an answer, and know that the figures you had in mind con- sisted of two and three, but the total of those figures wouldn't be ten."

"Apparently you want to point out that there's a factor I've missed somewhere, that there's an extra five I don't know about."

"Exactly," she said.

"And what makes you think there's this extra five? What have I missed?"

"The anonymous letter I received in the afternoon mail had been postmarked at five thirty p.m. *yesterday*. If you are the one who suggested the Royal Pheasant, how did someone know *yesterday* that you and Stella were to have a date there tonight?"

"All right, let's go," he told her. "There's a possibility the janitor hasn't cleaned up in your office. We're going to have to find that letter, put the torn pieces together, and recon- struct the postmark on that envelope. There's also the pos- sibility that your totals are all wrong and the postmark was a clever forgery. How come you noticed it?"

"Because Uncle Benedict told me if you ever wanted to get anywhere you had to notice details."

"Who's Uncle Benedict?"

"He's the black sheep of my family, the one who made his living by—" Abruptly she became silent. She realized all too keenly that she couldn't tell Don Kimberly about her Uncle Benedict. There were only a few people she *could* tell about him.

Kimberly signed both names to the register and said to the janitor, "Let's go up to E. B. Halsey's office, please, and make it snappy. Do you know whether that office has been cleaned?"

"Sure it has. We begin on that floor. That's the brass-hat floor. They're always out by five o'clock. Some of the other floors are later—"

"And you're certain Halsey's office has been cleaned up?"

"Sure. I did it myself."

"You emptied the wastebasket?"

"Yes."

"All right, we have to get that stuff. There was something in the wastebasket. Where is it now?"

The man grinned as he brought the elevator to a stop. "The stuff that was in that wastebasket is smoke by this time."

"You incinerated it?"

"Sure."

"I thought you sometimes saved it for a central pickup."

"No more, we don't. We burn it up. Everything in the wastebaskets is burned right here in the building. That's E. B. Halsey's orders. Don't let anything go out."

They hurried to E. B. Halsey's office. As the janitor had told them, it had been cleaned. The square mahogany colored wastebasket in Peggy Castle's secretarial office was completely free of paper. There was a folded square of cardboard in the bottom, and Peggy pulled it out in the vain hope that some fragment of the letter might have worked down beneath it.

There was nothing.

"I guess that's it," Kimberly said.

"Wait a minute," she told him. "I have a hunch. The way that janitor looked when he said the papers had been burned—come on."

The janitor evidently had been expecting their ring because he brought the cage up quickly.

"All done?" he asked.

"Not quite," Peggy said. "We want to go down to the basement. I want to see where you burn those papers."

"It's just an ordinary incinerator. Mr. Halsey said that he wanted all papers burned on the premises, and—"

"I'm checking," Peggy said. "It's something important. I think Mr. Halsey will want a report tomorrow."

"Oh."

The janitor stopped the cage at the basement and said, "Right over to the left."

Peggy all but ran down the passageway to where several big clothesbaskets were stacked in front of an incinerator. Two of the clothesbaskets were almost full.

"What's this?"

"Scraps that we haven't burned yet."

"I thought you told me everything had been burned."

"Well, everything from your office."

"How do you know what offices these came from?"

The man fidgeted uncomfortably. "Well, I *think* that these two came from the lower floors."

Peggy nodded to Kimberly, then upset the entire contents of the baskets on the floor, and started pawing through them, throwing to one side the envelopes, circular letters, newspapers, scratch paper—all the odds and ends that accumulate in a busy office.

"We don't need to look through anything that isn't torn," she said to Kimberly. "I tore this letter up into fine pieces. And you don't need to bother with anything that's typewritten. This was written in ink in longhand."

They tossed the larger pieces back into the clothesbaskets. When they had sifted the whole thing down to the smaller pieces, Peggy suddenly gave a triumphant exclamation. "This is part of it," she said, holding up a triangular section of paper.

"Then here's another part," Kimberly said.

"And here's another." She pounced on another piece.

Kimberly found a fourth. "This piece has part of the postmark on it," he said, fitting it together with the other pieces. "Gosh, you were right. It's postmarked yesterday at five thirty. But I tell you no one knew—"

Peggy caught his eye, glanced significantly at the janitor, who was watching them with an expression of puzzled speculation.

Kimberly nodded, and thereafter devoted his energies entirely to the search.

At last they were finished with the final scrap of paper on the floor. By this time they had recovered four pieces of the envelope and six pieces of the letter.

"I guess that's it," Peggy said. "Let's go up to the office and put these together."

Back in the office, with the aid of transparent tape, they fitted the pieces into a hopelessly inadequate reconstruction of a letter that Peggy now realized was undoubtedly destined to be of the greatest interest to the police.

The writer of that letter, Peggy knew, had it in her power to make Don Kimberly the Number One Suspect in the Stella Lynn murder.

Would the writer come forward? She doubted it, but she thought it was likely that, since one anonymous letter had been written to her, another would be written—but this time to the police.

And Peggy also realized that by falling in with Don Kimberly's highly abridged account of the evening's activities, she had nominated herself as Suspect Number Two if the police ever should learn exactly what had happened.

Peggy knew enough of E. B. Halsey's temperament to know that her future at WEFI depended on not letting the police find out all that had happened—at least for now.

E. B. Halsey, at 56, prided himself on his erect carriage, his keen eyes that needed spectacles only for reading, and his golf.

There were whispered stories about extracurricular activities. At times when he was with cronies whom he had known for years and whom he knew he could trust, it was understood Old E. B. could really let loose. There were rumors of certain wolfish tendencies he was supposed to have exhibited on rare occasion.

These last tendencies were the most delectable from the standpoint of powder-room discussion at WEFI, and the hardest to verify. Old E. B. was too shrewd ever to get caught off base. He took no chances on a rebuff, and any amatory affairs he may have indulged in were so carefully masked, so skillfully camouflaged, that the office rumors, although persistent, remained only rumors.

It was 9:30 when E. B. bustled into the office, jerked his head in a quick sparrowlike gesture, and said, "Good morning, Miss Castle," and then popped into his private office.

Ten seconds later he pressed the button that summoned Miss Castle.

That was typical of the man. He had undoubtedly arrived an hour early so he could ask what had happened the night before, but it would have been completely out of character for him to have said, "Good morning, Miss Castle. Would you mind stepping into my office?" He would instead enter his office, carefully place his hat on the shelf in the coat closet, stand for a few seconds in front of the mirror smoothing his hair, straightening his tie, and then, only then, would he settle himself in the big swivel chair at the polished-walnut desk and press the mother-of-pearl button that sounded Peggy's buzzer.

Peggy picked up her notebook, entered the office, and seated herself in a chair.

E.B. waved the notebook aside. "Never mind the notebook. I want to ask you a few questions."

She glanced up at him as though she hadn't been anticipating this interview for the past ten hours.

"You were with Kimberly last night?"

She nodded.

"That was a nasty piece in the paper. I don't like to have the company's name brought into prominence in connection with things of this sort. A company employee dead. Body found by two other employees who are out together. Possibility of murder. It gives the company a lot of bad publicity."

"I'm sorry," she said.

He cleared his throat. "You've done newspaper work?"

"A little, on a small paper."

"You have sense. I'm going to get another secretary. From now on you're going to be public relations counselor for this company. Your first job is to see that there's no more bad publicity of the sort that's in the papers this morning.

"Your new position carries with it a substantial increase in salary. You will, of course, keep on with your column in the house organ. I like the chatty humorous way you make the office gossip interesting, make employees sound important.

"No, no, don't thank me. This appointment is in the nature of a trial. I'll have to see what you can do to kill the sort of talk that we're sure to get about Stella Lynn's death. Now tell me what happened in detail."

He paused, peering at her over the top of his glasses as though she were in some way personally responsible for Stella Lynn's death.

Peggy Castle told him about the anonymous letter, about going to the Royal Pheasant, and her conversation with Don Kimberly.

"Then you weren't with Don Kimberly?" E. B. asked.

"Not in the sense of having a date with him."

"The papers say you had a dinner date. The police told me the same thing."

"That was a mistake."

E.B. pursed his lips. "Since they think you and Don Kimberly were on a date and merely dropped in on Stella on a friendly call, I think it would be better to let it stay that way."

"May I ask why?"

"It's better not to change a story that has appeared in the press. It puts you in a bad position."

"The mistake was made by the police in assuming we were out together."

E. B. beamed at her. "So that leaves us with a clear conscience, eh? All right, we'll leave it that you and Don had a dinner date."

"But that story won't hold up. The headwaiter knows we didn't come in together; so do the table waiters."

E. B. frowned, then yielded the point reluctantly. "Very

well, then, I suppose you'll have to tell them the truth."

Peggy waited. She had said nothing of the jeweled butterfly she had taken from Stella's stocking.

E. B. put the tips of his fingers together. "The pieces of the letter?" he asked.

"I have them in my desk."

"I think we'd better take a look," he said.

She brought them in to him.

"You're sure these pieces are from the envelope?"

"Yes. You can see the handwriting is the same, and this was the only handwritten letter addressed to me in the afternoon mail."

E. B. thoughtfully poked at the pieces of paper.

"How does Kimberly explain this letter?" he asked abruptly.

"He doesn't. He can't."

The telephone on E. B.'s desk rang sharply three times.

E.B. picked up the receiver and said, "Yes. E.B. Halsey."

He frowned for a moment, then said, "This call should have gone to Miss Castle's desk in the ordinary way. However—yes, I understand.... Very well, I'll see him. Yes, bring him down here."

Halsey hung up the telephone and once more looked at Peggy over his glasses. "A Detective Nelson is out there. Know anything about him?"

"No."

"He wants to talk with me. The receptionist became flustered and rang me personally. The call should have gone through your office. However, the damage is done now. I don't want to antagonize the police in any way. You might step out to receive him."

She nodded and went to the reception room just as the receptionist held the door open for E. B.'s visitor.

He wasn't the type she had expected. He might have been a successful accountant or a bond salesman. He was slender, quietly dressed, and when he spoke his voice was melodious.

"I'm Fred Nelson," he said, "from headquarters."

He was holding a card case in his hand as though expecting to be called on to produce credentials. He exhibited a gold shield and gave Peggy a card, a neatly embossed card with a police shield in gold in the upper left-hand corner.

"Mr. Halsey is expecting you."

"You're his secretary, Miss Castle?"

"That's right."

"I think I want to see you both," he said. "I believe you and your escort discovered the body."

"I was with Mr. Kimberly."

He nodded.

"Do you wish to see Mr. Kimberly at the same time?" she asked.

He shook his head. "Just you and Mr. Halsey."

"Will you step this way, please."

She ushered him into Halsey's office. Nelson shook hands with E. B. and said, "I took the liberty of asking your secretary to remain during the interview, Mr. Halsey."

E. B. beamed at him. "That's fine. Quite all right. Sit right down. Anything we can do for you we'll be glad to do. A most unfortunate occurrence. Always hate to have these tragedies. We're something like a big family here and these things cut pretty close to home."

"You knew Miss Lynn on a personal basis, then?" Nelson asked.

E. B.'s steady eyes surveyed the detective over the top of his glasses. He hesitated for approximately two seconds as though debating just how to answer the detective's question, then said curtly, "Yes."

"Had you known Miss Lynn before she came to work here?"

"That is the point I was about to bring up," Halsey said.

"Go ahead. Bring it up."

"I knew Miss Lynn before she came to this city. As a matter of fact, she asked me about a position and I told her that I would be glad to refer her to the head of our personnel department and suggest that other things being equal—you understand, Mr. Nelson?"

Nelson nodded.

"—other things being equal," Halsey went on, "I'd like to have her taken on. Of course, in a business the size of this

148

the personnel department handles the entire thing. They know the vacancies and the abilities that are required. They have, I believe, tests for—"

"The point is that you interceded for her with the personnel department and Stella Lynn got a job?"

"That's putting it in a rather peculiar way."

Nelson turned to Peggy. "Did Stella Lynn seemed to be brooding, worried, apprehensive?"

"I didn't know her well, Mr. Nelson. I saw her off and on and chatted with her when I saw her. She was always cheerful. I'd say she was probably the least likely candidate for suicide—"

"I wasn't thinking about suicide."

"Well, a person doesn't worry about murder."

"I wasn't thinking about murder."

E. B. cleared his throat. "Well, then, may I ask what you *were* thinking about?"

Nelson glanced at Peggy Castle. "Something else," he said. "Something Miss Lynn could well have worried about."

"Good Lord," Peggy said impatiently, "I understand English, and I understand the facts of life. Are you trying to tell us that she was pregnant?"

Nelson nodded.

E. B. put his elbows on the desk, his chin in his hands. "Good Lord!" he murmured.

"You seem upset," Nelson said.

"He's thinking of the good name of the company," Peggy explained, "—of the publicity."

"Oh, I see," Nelson said in a dry voice. He turned to Peggy. "I'd like to have your story, Miss Castle, right from the beginning."

"There isn't any story. Mr. Kimberly and I decided to look in on Stella Lynn, and we found her lying dead on the floor. We called the police."

"That certainly is a succinct statement," Nelson said.

"I don't know how I could elaborate on it."

"You didn't know Stella Lynn well?"

"Not particularly well, no."

"How did it happen that you went to call on her, then?"

"It was Mr. Kimberly's suggestion."

"And why did he want to call on her last night?"

She said, "I'm afraid Mr. Kimberly doesn't think it necessary to confide in me."

"Perhaps he'll be a little less reticent with *me*," Nelson said.

"Perhaps."

Nelson turned toward the door. "Well, I just wanted to find out what you knew about Stella Lynn's background," he said. "I'll talk with Kimberly, and then I'll be back."

He walked out without a word of farewell.

As the door closed, E. B. picked up the telephone and said to the receptionist, "A man by the name of Nelson is leaving my office. He wants to see Mr. Kimberly. I want him to be delayed until I can get Kimberly on the phone and— What's that? . . . Oh, I see. . . . Well, that explains it. All right."

E. B. hung up, looked at Peggy, and said, "That's why he didn't ask to have Kimberly in on our conference. Mr. Kimberly is not in the office this morning. No one seems to know where he is."

He paused for a moment, digesting that information, then said, "Of course, that is a temporary expedient. It gives him a certain margin of time—I notice you didn't tell Detective Nelson about that letter, Miss Castle."

"I couldn't."

"Why not?"

"It doesn't fit in with Kimberly's version of what happened. Kimberly says Stella Lynn called him up around ten thirty in the morning and told him that she had to see him. He's the one who suggested the Royal Pheasant. Yet this letter, which was postmarked the day before, informed me that Kimberly and Stella Lynn were going to be dining at the Royal Pheasant."

E. B. regarded Peggy thoughtfully for a moment. "You have a remarkably shrewd mind, Miss Castle."

She flushed. "Thank you."

"Now, just what do you have in your mind?"

She said, "Stella Lynn's desk. I'd like to clean it out. She'll have some private stuff in there. I'd like to look through it before the police do. No one has said anything about—"

"A splendid idea," E. B. said. "Get busy. And don't tell me what you're doing. I'd prefer not to know *all* the steps you're taking. That desk, for instance. In case you should find a diary or something—well, you'll know what to do."

E. B. regarded her over the tops of his glasses. "I'm *sure* you'll know what to do."

Peggy placed a cardboard carton on top of Stella Lynn's desk and began to clean out the drawers, fully realizing that the typists at the adjoining desks were making a surreptitious check on all her actions.

There was an old magazine, a pair of comfortable shoes to be worn at work, a paper bag containing a pair of new nylons, a receipt for rent on her apartment, a small camera in a case, and a half-empty package of tissues.

There was no diary. But there was a disarray of the drawers, as if they might have been hurriedly searched at an earlier hour.

Peggy wondered what had led E. B. to believe there might be a diary in the desk. She dumped the contents of the desk into the carton, tied the carton with heavy string, and then, with a crayon, printed the name *Stella Lynn* on the side. Having done all this to impress the typists at adjoining desks, Peggy carried the carton back to her own office.

When the door was safely closed she opened the package and inspected the camera. The figure "10" appeared through the little circular window on the back of the camera, indicating that nine pictures had been taken.

Peggy turned the knob until the roll had been transferred to the take-up spool, removed it from the camera, and carefully wiped off the camera to remove her fingerprints. She slipped the camera back into its case, put the case into the carton, tied the carton up with string, and stepped to the door of E. B.'s private office.

She tapped on the door. When she received no answer, she tried the knob; it turned and she gently opened the door.

E. B. was not in his office.

She went back to her desk. A piece of paper that had been pushed under the blotter caught her eye. She pulled it out.

It was a note from E. B., scrawled hastily.

Miss Castle:

As soon as you left my office I recalled an urgent matter that had escaped my attention in the excitement over the interruption of our regular morning program. It is a matter of greatest importance and must be kept entirely confidential. I am working on that matter and expect to be out of the office for some time. I will get in touch with you as soon as I have a definite schedule. In the meantime I will be unavailable.

It was signed with the initials *E. B.*

Peggy looked at it. "Well," she said, "Kimberly and Halsey. That makes it unanimous."

Peggy batted her eyes and turned her most charming manner on Mrs. Maxwell, the apartment-house manager.

"I certainly hope you don't think I'm too ghoulish, Mrs. Maxwell, but, after all, a girl has to live."

Mrs. Maxwell nodded almost imperceptibly, studying her visitor through narrowed eyes around which pools of flesh had been deposited so that the eyes seemed to be about half normal size. Her hair had been dyed a brilliant orange-red, and her cheeks had been rouged too heavily.

"Apartments are *so* hard to get," Peggy went on, "and, of course, I read in the paper about Stella Lynn's unfortunate death. So I know that the apartment is untenanted, and I know that you're going to have to rent it. Some people might be superstitious about moving into an apartment of that sort, but I definitely am not, and, well, I thought I'd like to be the first applicant."

Again the nod was all but imperceptible.

"I'm not too well fixed," Peggy said. "I'm an honest working girl, and I don't have any—protector—in the background, but I do have fifty dollars saved up that I'd planned to use as a bonus in getting exactly the right kind of apartment. If this apartment suits me, since I wouldn't have any need for the bonus, I'll give it to you in gratitude for the personal inconvenience of showing me the apartment."

This time the nod of the head was definitely more pronounced, then Mrs. Maxwell said, "My hands are tied right at the moment."

"In what way?"

"I can't get in to show the apartment."

"Oh, surely you have a key—"

"The police have put a seal on both doors, front and back. They've been looking for fingerprints—"

"Fingerprints!" Peggy exclaimed. "What do they expect to find out from fingerprints?"

"I don't know. They've put powder over the whole apartment. They've ordered me to keep out. They've sealed up the doors so they can't be opened without breaking the seal."

"Well, you can tell me about the apartment?"

"Oh, yes."

"How about milk?"

"Milk can be delivered at the back."

"And the collection of garbage and cans?"

"There are two receptacles, one for cans and glass, one for garbage. The garbage is collected every other day, the cans and glass twice a week. The tenant has to deposit the material in receptacles on the ground floor in the back."

"I believe this apartment is on the fifth floor."

"That's right."

"I have to walk down five flights of stairs to—"

"Four flights, dearie."

"Well, four flights of stairs to deposit cans and garbage?"

"I'm sorry. There isn't any dumbwaiter service."

"May I take a look at the back stairs?"

"Certainly. Just go through that door at the end of the corridor. Look around all you want, dearie."

When the going got tough, Peggy Castle sometimes appealed for help to her Great-uncle Benedict.

Benedict Castle had lived a highly checkered career. One of Peggy's earliest memories was of hearing the mellifluous voice of Uncle Benedict reminiscently extolling the virtues of Benedict's Body Builder.

". . . Not a chemical, ladies and gentlemen, that tries to achieve health by whipping the worn glands, the tired muscles, the jaded nerves to greater and greater effort until finally the whole machine breaks down, but a tonic, ladies and gentlemen, that helps Mother Nature *renew* worn glands, *create* new cells, *build* new muscles, and *make* new blood. Now, who's going to be the first to get one of these bottles of B.B.B., offered tonight not at the regular price of ten dollars, not even at the half price of five dollars but at the ludicrously low price of one dollar! Only one dollar to build the body into *renewed* health!"

That had been 20 years before. Peggy, four years old, had been an orphan—too young to appreciate the tragedy that had deprived her of both father and mother—an orphan picked up and raised as their own child by Uncle Benedict and Aunt Martha.

The days of the patent medicine vender had long passed, but Uncle Benedict loved to review the patter he had used in his prime, the patter that had enabled him to travel around, living, as he expressed it, "on the fat of the yokels." It was before the days of Federal Trade Commission supervision, the Pure Food and Drug Act, and the income tax.

Uncle Benedict had had a horse-drawn van that by day served as living quarters and laboratory, at night opened to provide a stage on which his magic fingers performed feats of sleight of hand while his magic tongue brought in a steady stream of silver coins on which there was no income tax and no necessity to account to anyone.

No one knew how much Uncle Benedict took in. He went where he wished, did what he wished, and spent his money as he wished.

When the patent medicine business began to die, other infinitely more lucrative fields opened up. It was the era of mining stock and the wildcat oil speculator. Gradually Uncle Benedict drifted into a gang of clever sharpshooters, a gang in which Uncle Benedict was referred to as "The Sleeper." Never was there another man who could put on such a convincing act of sleeping while his ballbearing mind was working out plans for fleecing suckers.

Uncle Benedict was at his best in the club car of a transcontinental train. He'd sit down, drink a beer, then let his head droop forward in gentle audible slumber. People sitting next to him would discuss their business affairs with enough detail so that Uncle Benedict could figure out the correct approach.

Then Uncle Benedict would give a convulsive nod, a rather loud snore, waken with such evident embarrassment and look around him with such a panic-stricken apology for his snoring that the whole carful of people would spontaneously break into laughter.

After that Uncle Benedict was right at home.

Some ten years before, twinges of pain had announced the coming of arthritis. Gradually the long slender fingers that had been able to deal cards so convincingly from the bottom of the deck, or pick pockets with such consummate skill that a wallet could be lifted, carefully examined, and returned to its proper place, all without the sucker's having the faintest idea that he had been "cased"—gradually the nimble fingers began to thicken at the joints.

Now Uncle Benedict, confined to a wheel chair, dozed through the twilight of life, his mind as keenly active as ever, and even Martha, his wife, was unable to tell when his dozing was genuine slumber or when he was merely keeping his old act in practice.

Those who had known Uncle Benedict never forgot him. His friends worshipped the ground he walked on. It was a matter of police record that on three occasions suckers whom he had fleeced had refused to prosecute, stating publicly that they valued their brief companionship with Uncle Benedict far more than the money he had taken from them.

One of his victims had even gone so far as to place an ad in the personal column reading: *Dear Benedict, Come home. All is forgiven. We like you even if it did cost us money. . . .*

Not even Martha knew the ramifications of Uncle Benedict's connections. With a photographic memory for names, faces, and telephone numbers, Uncle Benedict kept no written memoranda. From time to time he would arouse himself from what seemed to be a sound sleep, send his wheel chair scurrying across to the telephone, dial a number, and give cryptic instructions. Occasionally men came to the house, men who regarded Uncle Benedict's slightest word as law, men who shook hands very gently so as not to bring pain to the thickened joints, men who left envelopes containing crisp green currency.

The envelopes went in the wastebasket, the currency went into Uncle Benedict's pocket.

"Income tax!" he'd snort, when Aunt Martha asked him about his business affairs. "You don't pay income tax on gifts. That's a free-will offering." And that was all anybody ever got out of him.

Only once had he elaborated. He explained to Martha, "I showed a man how to make some money. I thought out a scheme. I picked the one man who could put that scheme into operation. When the scheme paid off he sent me a gift. You couldn't report a gift like that to the income tax. I didn't even count the money. That would have been looking a gift horse in the mouth."

Aunt Martha answered Peggy's ring. "Why, hello, Peggy. What on earth are *you* doing?"

"I'm up to my neck," Peggy said.

"I read in the papers that you discovered the body of a girl who'd died from poison."

"That's right."

"Well, for heaven's sake, let's not stand here gassing. Come on in."

Aunt Martha had for years been Uncle Benedict's "assistant," the assistance consisting of wearing a pair of skin-fitting black tights, a skirt that fell barely below the hips, a plunging neckline, and a fixed smile.

When Uncle Benedict had come to the point in one of his exhibitions where it was necessary to make a swift substitution or a few passes with the hand that he wanted to be invisible to the audience, Martha would "spontaneously" wiggle her hips, the fixed smile would become broader and more animate, and then the hip motion would swing into a rhythm of pure vivaciousness. As Uncle Benedict used to describe it, "It gave me the opportunity to do the trick, but by the time I'd got it done, half of the audience just didn't give a damn. They kept on watching Martha's hips."

"How's the old warrior?" Peggy asked.

Aunt Martha looked into the living room and said, "He's sound asleep, or thinking out a new scheme. I never know which."

The Sleeper was sitting in his chair, head drooping forward and slightly to one side. He was gently snoring. Abruptly he jerked into conscious wakefulness, choking off an extra loud snore in the middle. He looked at Peggy with every sign of embarrassment. "Good Lord, Peggy, how long have you been here?"

Peggy knew from the sheer perfection of his act that the old Sleeper had merely been keeping in practice.

"Uncle Benedict, I'm in a pint of trouble."

"That ain't so much trouble," Benedict said.

"I've been holding out on the police."

"Well, why not? You can't go around blabbing *all* you know."

She told him the whole story, and he listened carefully. "What do you want?" he asked when she had finished.

She said, "In the can receptacle for apartment five-nineteen are the broken remnants of a whiskey bottle. I want that salvaged before the can collector gets it. I want to have it processed for fingerprints, and then I want the latent prints photographed and preserved so they can be used as evidence at any time."

"What else do you want?"

"Your immoral support."

Uncle Benedict sent his wheel chair gliding over to the telephone. He dialed a number, waited, then said, "George?"

He waited a moment, then gave the address of the apartment house where Stella Lynn had lived. "There's a broken whiskey bottle in a galvanized receptacle in the back yard with the number five-nineteen on the can. I want that broken bottle carefully preserved. Dust it for fingerprints. Fix any prints you find so they'll stay there a long time. I also want 'em photographed.

"Now, you'd better have somebody with you to be a wit-

157

ness in case you're called on to make an identification of that bottle. Your record ain't so good. . . . Who's that? . . . Yes, he'll be fine. . . . If anybody says anything, flash a badge showing you're a sanitary inspector, and make a kick about some of the regulations being broken. . . . That's right, get them on the defensive. . . . Okay, let me know when you have it. Goodbye."

Uncle Benedict hung up and turned to Peggy. "That's taken care of. If you should need anything else let me know." His eyelids drooped and his head nodded.

Peggy took elaborate precautions to see that no one was following her and then called for the pictures she had left for a rush job.

In the privacy of her apartment she studied the nine pictures and was utterly disappointed. One picture at the beach showed a handsome young man in tight bathing trunks. He had blond wavy hair, an attractive smile, and a magnificent physique, but he meant nothing to Peggy.

There was a shot of an automobile parked by the beach; two pictures of Stella Lynn in a bathing suit that would never have passed any censor anywhere at any time. The bathing suit had evidently been concocted by knotting three bandanas carefully arranged so that they showed all the curves of her figure. It was a suit that was not intended to have any contact with the water.

There was a picture showing the back of an automobile, with a young man lifting two suitcases from the trunk. A series of small cabins with garages showed in the background of this picture.

Peggy looked for the license number on the automobile. Unfortunately the man was standing so that he concealed all but the last three figures—861.

Peggy studied a picture of a parked car with a stretch of beach in the background. Here again there was no opportunity to get any part of the license number. The car was shown sideways.

There was a picture of a picnic lunch spread out on the beach. The young man with the slender waist and square shoulders was seated cross-legged.

The telephone rang, and Peggy answered it.

Don Kimberly's voice said, "Thank heaven I've caught you, Peggy."

"What's the matter?"

"I got up to the office this morning and learned that a police detective was looking for me. I thought we should find out a little more about that letter before I talked with anyone, so I've been hiding out, but I didn't want to hide from you, and I didn't want you to think that I'd left you to stand the gaff. I've been trying to get you all day."

She felt a big surge of relief. "Oh, that's fine, Don," she said. "I'm glad you thought of me. Where are you now?"

"Right at the moment," he said, "I'm at a pay telephone."

She said, "I understand you're quite a photographer."

"I do quite a bit of photographic work, yes."

"I have some pictures that I think should be—well, I think we should enlarge one or two of them."

"Where did you get them?"

She was silent.

Kimberly said, "Oh-oh, I get it."

"How long will it take to do it?"

"How many are there?"

"Nine. But I think only two or three are important."

"Nothing to it," he said. "We could make enlargements just as big as you want, or pick out the part of the photo you wanted enlarged, and then we could go out to dinner. By the time we got back, the enlargements would be dry and we could study them carefully."

"Could you do all that yourself?"

"Sure. I'm all fixed up for it. I'll come around and get you."

"All right, but give me half an hour to shower and dress."

"Thirty minutes on the dot, and I'll be there," he said.

Peggy hung up and dashed for the shower, experiencing a peculiar feeling of exultation that Don hadn't left her to face the problems alone.

Don Kimberly showed Peggy around his apartment with a sense of pride, pointing out the framed photographs on the walls.

"You took all these?" she asked.

"All of them," he said. "I like dramatic cloud effects. You can see from these pictures that I've gone in for thunderheads and storms over the ocean. Of course, you deliberately dramatize that stuff by overcorrecting with a red filter, but it gives you a sense of power, of the forces of nature."

"It's wonderful," she said. "They're—they're believable. They're true. They somehow symbolize life."

"I'm glad you like them. Want to see the darkroom now?"

"I'd love to."

"Let's take a look at those films, Peggy."

She handed him the envelope. He brushed the prints aside and studied the negatives.

"Well," he said, "the girl used an expensive camera."

"How do you know without seeing it?"

"You can tell by the films," he said. "The films are wire sharp. That means she had a coupled range finder and a high-grade lens. That's why I like to look at negatives instead of prints. The negatives tell the story. Lots of times a cheaper lens will give you a warm black that makes the print seem all right, but the minute you start to blow it up it fuzzes out on you. We'll make some enlargements right away."

"Where's the darkroom?" she asked.

He laughed. "This is a bachelor apartment. There was a big pantry off the kitchen, a lot bigger than I needed, so I made it lightproof, installed running water, and fixed up a darkroom. Come on in and I'll show you my workshop."

He led the way into the darkroom and showed Peggy the two enlarging cameras. One of them used what he called "cold light," and the other used condensers for sharpness of detail.

Kimberly poured chemicals into stainless-steel trays. "We'll have these pictures enlarged in a jiffy. Why so thoughtful, Peggy?"

"Because I want to ask you something that's probably none of my business."

"What?"

"You know of Stella's condition?"

"Yes."

"Were you—" she asked, "that is—were you—"

"You mean am I the man in the case?"

"Yes."

"No." He was silent for a few moments. Then he added, "I've known Stella for years. She was working in a cafeteria when I first knew her. She was a good-natured, lovable kid. I saw her a few times. Then someone put me on a committee to pick the queen of some local festivities. There was a lineup of a lot of girls in bathing suits, and to my surprise I saw Stella Lynn in the lineup.

"I don't think the fact that I knew her influenced my judgment. Anyway, I voted for her, and so did the other two judges. She was elected queen of the outfit. That was three years ago. She's put on weight since then, but at that time—well, she had a *good* figure."

"Go ahead," Peggy said, then added, "that is, if you want to."

"I want to. I want you to know what the situation was. Stella rang me up to thank me for voting for her, and I congratulated her on winning the contest on sheer merit. Then I lost track of her for a while. Then she rang up again and said she wanted to get away from the small town, wanted to go to the city. I gathered there had been a heartbreak."

"That's the part I wanted to know about," Peggy said.

"Why?"

"Because I'm trying to reconstruct Stella's life."

"Actually," Don Kimberly said, "I don't know too much about her background, Peggy. Do you believe that?"

"Of course."

"There are some who won't," he said thoughtfully. "However, to get back to your question. She was in love with someone. I don't know who he was, but I have an idea he was a no-good. Stella wanted to get out of town. She was pretty well broken up, and she was broke financially. I had to lend her money to clean up a few bills she had around Cofferville and help her get started on a new job. I had no idea her new job was in our company until I met her there."

"E. B. Halsey fixed that up for her," she said.

"I know E. B. knew her dad in Cofferville. He's been dead some five years, but E. B. knew him and liked him."

"And knew her?"

"Apparently."

"How well?"

"I don't know. Stella never talked about her friends. I've been trying to contact E. B. He isn't available."

"I know. This money you lent her, Don—did she pay it back?"

"Yes. Why?"

"She needed a lump sum. You gave her a check?"

"Yes."

"But when she paid you back it must have been just a little here and a little there in cash."

"It was."

"Then she didn't have anything to show that she paid you?"

"Are you suggesting I'd try to make her pay twice?"

"I'm thinking of the way the police will look at it," she said. "The banks keep records on microfilm of all checks that pass through their hands."

"I know," he said curtly, and she could tell that he was worried.

The doorbell rang sharply, insistently.

Kimberly looked at her in dismay. "I was hoping we could have a chance to get together on a story before—I'll have to answer it, Peggy, particularly since you're here."

He led the way out of the darkroom and opened the front door.

Detective Fred Nelson and a young woman stood at the door. "Hello, Kimberly," Nelson said easily. "This is Frances Bushnell—in case that means anything to you."

Don Kimberly, without inviting them in, said, "How do you do, Miss Bushnell."

"It's Mrs. Bushnell," Nelson said. "We're coming in, Kimberly." He pushed past Kimberly, saw Peggy, and said,

"Well, well, it seems the gang's all here. Sit down, folks."

"Since you're playing the part of host," Kimberly said coldly, "perhaps you'd like to mix some drinks?"

"Now, keep your shirt on," Nelson told him. "This is business. I'm going to be brief. Mrs. Bushnell was a close friend of Stella Lynn's. She and her husband and Stella's boy friend used to go out on foursomes. Tell them about those foursomes, Frances."

Frances Bushnell seemed ill at ease.

"Go on," Nelson said, "get it off your chest. Don't pull any punches. We may as well find out where we stand now as later."

"Well," Mrs. Bushnell said, and paused to clear her throat as though not quite certain of herself. "Pete, that was my husband—he still is—and Stella, and Bill Everett—"

"Now, who is Bill Everett?" Nelson interrupted.

"That was Stella's boy friend."

"And when was this?"

"When she was in Cofferville, working in the cafeteria as cashier."

"All right, go ahead."

"Well, Pete and I and Stella and Bill used to go out on weekends together. We were all friends. Pete and I got married. I got to know Stella quite well."

"What about this Bill guy?" Nelson asked.

"He turned out to be no good. I think he got into some trouble somewhere. I know it broke Stella's heart. I think she was really fond of him."

"How long ago was this?"

"About two years ago."

"Then what?"

"Pete and I got married and came here to live. When Stella came she looked us up. I still kept in touch with her."

"Now, when was the last time you saw her?"

"Yesterday afternoon."

"Where?"

"In a cocktail bar on Fifth Street."

"You just happened to run into her, or did you have an

appointment, or what?"

"It's a sort of gathering place. Some of us girls who work in offices drop in for a little chat and a cocktail. Stella was there."

"What did she say?"

"Well, we talked for a while about this and that and I asked her if she wanted to have dinner with me and she said no, that she had a dinner date with a Prince Charming who was taking her to a night spot—that she had something to tell him that was going to jolt him."

"Did she tell you the man's name?"

"Yes."

"What was it?"

"Don Kimberly." .

"Did she tell you she was going to let him know he was about to become a father?"

"She said she was going to tell him something that was going to jolt him."

Nelson turned to Kimberly. "Thought you'd like to hear this," he said. "In view of Mrs. Bushnell's story I think I'll take a look around—unless, of course, you have some objection. If you do, I'll get a warrant and look anyway."

"I see," Kimberly said sarcastically. "The good old police system. If you can't solve a crime, start trying to pin it on someone."

"Who said anybody was trying to pin anything on you?"

"You might as well have said it," Kimberly blazed. "Go right ahead. Look through the place. I'll just go along with you to make sure you don't plant anything."

"Now, is that nice?" Nelson asked. He got up and walked around the living room, then pointed to a door and asked, "What's this?"

"Bedroom," Kimberly said curtly.

Nelson went in. The others followed him. Nelson looked around, opened the door of the clothes closet, carefully studied the clothes, looked into the bathroom, and gave particular attention to the bottles in the medicine cabinet.

Then he went into the kitchen, pointed to another door, and asked, "What's that?"

"Darkroom."

Nelson pushed in. The others stood in the doorway. Nelson said, "You have your amber light on; you're all set up for something."

"Yes, I was doing a little enlarging."

"He was showing me something about photography," Peggy said.

"I see," Nelson said in a tone of voice that indicated his mind was far away. He began opening the various bottles on the shelves and smelling the contents. He said, "I do quite a bit of photography myself. You've got a little more expensive equipment here than I can afford. That's a swell enlarger. You like the condensers better than the cold light?"

Kimberly made no answer.

Nelson whistled a tune as he moved around the darkroom, looking over the bottles, studying the labels, smelling the contents.

Suddenly he paused. "What the hell's this?" he asked.

"Potassium bromide. If you're a photographer you should know."

"The hell it is. That stuff comes in large crystals. This is—smell it."

"I don't think it has any odor," Kimberly said.

"Well, this stuff does. Take a smell. And don't get your nose too close to it. You might wish you hadn't."

Kimberly sniffed the bottle gingerly, then turned puzzled eyes toward the detective. "Why," he said, "that smells—smells like—"

"Exactly," Nelson agreed. "It smells like potassium cyanide. It *is* potassium cyanide."

Abruptly he put the bottle down, put the cork back in place, and said, "I don't want anyone to touch that bottle. I'm going to process it for fingerprints. I left my fingerprints around the neck of the bottle, but I didn't leave them on the rest of it. And now, Mr. Donald Kimberly, I'm sorry, but I'm arresting you for the murder of Stella Lynn."

In a taxicab headed toward Uncle Benedict's, Peggy studied the purloined pictures, trying to penetrate the details of the shadows.

Don Kimberly's arrest had been a terrific shock. The statement of Mrs. Bushnell had been like a devastating bomb.

Peggy had a blind faith in Don Kimberly, but she couldn't combat his arrest except by digging up new and convincing evidence. The morning newspapers would sound the death knell of her new job unless something could be turned up. She hoped her uncle had been able to get some fingerprints from that broken whiskey bottle.

The beach scene, Peggy concluded, was a picnic, and apparently it had been a twosome—just Stella Lynn and the young man in the bathing suit who appeared in the pictures. He had taken a couple of pictures of Stella. The costume Stella was wearing would not have been permitted on a public beach, so these pictures must have been taken at a private part of the beach. Had they been taken before the others or afterward?

The series of small cabins, all uniform in appearance, suggested a motel, probably somewhere along the beach.

The cab slowed to a stop at Uncle Benedict's. "Wait for me," she told the driver, and ran up the steps.

Aunt Martha came to the door. "Heaven's sake, Peggy, give a body a chance to get there. You rang three times while I was putting my knitting down. What's the trouble?"

"Nothing. Where's Uncle?"

"Right here. Come on in."

Peggy walked over to the wheel chair and kissed Benedict on the forehead.

"What's the trouble?" he asked.

"Nothing in particular but I wanted to see if you'd found out anything about that broken bottle and—"

"Damn it, Peggy," he said irritably, "I've taught you to lie better than that."

"What's wrong?" she asked.

"Everything. Never run your words together when you're lying. Sounds too much like reciting a formula. Never let a sucker feel he's hearing a rehearsed line. When you're lying you want to be thoroughly at ease—never have tension in your voice.

"Keep your sentences short. Don't intersperse explanations with lies. That's where the average liar falls down. He puts himself on the defensive in the middle of what should be the most convincing part of his lie.

"Now sit down and tell me what's handed you such a jolt. Tell the truth, if you can. If you can't, tell the kind of lie that'll make me proud of you. Now, what's up?"

Peggy said, "They arrested Don Kimberly for Stella's murder."

"What evidence?"

"That's the tough part. They found a bottle of potassium cyanide among his photographic chemicals, right over the sink in his darkroom."

Uncle Benedict threw back his grizzled head and laughed.

"It's no laughing matter," she said.

"Makes him out so damned stupid, that's all. There he is with a whole darkroom. Got a sink and running water and everything, eh?"

"That's right."

"How many more people did they think he was aiming to kill with cyanide?"

"What do you mean?"

"Suppose he had killed her. He's scored a bull's-eye. That was all he wanted. He'd done the job. He's got no more use for poison. He'd wash the rest of it down the drain.

"Nope, somebody's planting evidence. Seems funny the cops didn't think about that. Perhaps they have. Maybe they're giving this person lots of rope for self-hanging purposes."

Listening to him, she realized the logic of what he said, and suddenly felt much better. She spread the pictures out in front of him.

Uncle Benedict's eyes lit up. "Good-looking babe," he said, studying the pictures of Stella in the bathing suit. "Darn good-looking."

Aunt Martha, fixing a pot of hot tea for Peggy, snorted, "You'd think he was a Don Juan to listen to him."

"Casanova, Casanova," Uncle Benedict corrected her irritably. "All right, what about these pictures, Peggy?"

"What can you tell me about them?"

He picked up the pictures and studied them. Then he said, "This is the motel where they stayed Saturday."

"Who stayed there?"

"This girl in a bathing suit and the fellow who's with her."

"Uncle Benedict, you shouldn't say things like that without knowing. You don't know they *stayed* there, and you can't *know* it was Saturday."

"I don't, eh?" he grinned. "It sticks out plain as the nose on your face. This picture with the beach in the background was taken Sunday morning. Same car here as in the other picture. Put two and two together."

"You're jumping at conclusions and not being very fair to Stella."

"Not as bad as what the coroner did, broadcasting a girl's secrets that way. Ought to be ashamed of himself. Two months' pregnant, and he puts it in the paper!"

"He had to do that," she said. "It's part of the evidence. It shows the motivation for murder."

"Uh-huh," Uncle Benedict said.

"What makes you think it was Saturday noon in one picture and Sunday morning in the other?" she asked.

"Use your eyes," he told her. "Here's a motel. See all those garages with cars in them?"

"Yes."

"Where's the sun?"

"What do you mean, where's the sun?"

"Look at your shadows," he said. "Here, hand me that ruler."

She handed it to him. His arthritis-crippled hands moved the ruler over the photograph so that one end was against a patch of shadow, the other end against the top of an ornamental light pole. "All right, there's the angle of your sun, good and high."

"All right, so what?"

"Look at the automobiles in the garages. Most motel patrons are transients. They're hitting the road. They want to come in at night, have a bath, sleep, get up early, be on their way.

"Now, look at this one. Automobiles in almost every ga-rage, and from the angle of the sun it's either three in the afternoon or nine in the morning. Look carefully, and you can see it's morning because here's a cabin with a key in a half-open door. The key has a big metal tag hanging from it so tenants won't cart it off, and it's caught the sunlight and reflected it right into the camera. That car got away early. If it had been afternoon the key would have been in the office instead of the door.

"Only one car is gone; most of the people using the motel aren't traveling and that means it's Sunday. The guests are weekenders, people who came Saturday to spend a weekend. Spend it where? Not in a motel, unless that motel's at a beach.

"Now, look at this one. Automobiles in almost every ga-rage, and from the angle of the sun it's either three in the men on it. Those are people who came early and—"

"I don't see any wharf."

"Take a good look," he said.

"That's just a black spot out there—no, wait a minute—"

"Black spot nothing," he said. "It's the end of a pier. See sticking out there? Take a magnifying glass; you'll see people all bunched up, fishing at the far end of the—"

"Of course," she said. "I hadn't noticed it before."

"Now, look at the people. Here's where a road runs down to the beach. Jammed with cars parked all along it. But people haven't spread out on the north end of the beach yet. On a Sunday the whole thing would be crowded. The way it is now, just about the number of people are on the beach who would have come in those parked cars. They haven't had to park their cars way uptown and walk down to the beach.

"See the shadow of the automobile? Sun's pretty much overhead. It's just about noon. Wouldn't get that big a play on a beach this time of year except Saturday. Sunday noon 'd be even bigger. All right, what more do you want to know?"

She said, "I'd like to know who owns that automobile."

"Why don't you find out?"

"How can I?"

He said, "How many beaches are there around here tha[t] have piers sticking out that far? How many motels in tha[t] city—"

"What city?"

He tapped the ornamental lighting fixture. "See th[e] peculiar design on that lighting fixture? I could tell you [a] lot about those fixtures. Pal of mine took over the sale [of] ornamental lighting fixtures to a city. *There's* a great op[-]portunity! That's *real* graft. Perfectly legitimate. I gues[s] that's why I never cared much for it, but I can tell you—"

"You don't have to tell me," she said, "I know where it [is] myself now. Why in the world didn't I notice the signif[i-]cance of that ornamental street light before?"

"Preoccupied," he said. "That's 'cause you're in love."

"I am not!"

"Bet you are! Wrapped up in that Beau Brummell gu[y] they took to prison."

"I am not, but—I *would* like to impress him once wit[h] Peggy Castle the girl and not just Peggy Castle the logic[al] thinker."

"How are you going to do it?"

"I'm going to prove he didn't commit the murder."

Uncle Benedict chuckled. "Listen to her, Martha. Sh[e] wants him to notice her as a cute trick and not as an ef[fi-]cient thinking machine, so she goes out and uses her *brai[n]*. Don't use your brain when you're trying to impress a ma[n], Peggy. Don't let him think you have any brain. Ha[ve] curves. Be helpless and—"

"You leave Peggy alone," Aunt Martha said. "She's doi[ng] it her way."

Uncle Benedict shook his head. "Men can't see glam[or] and brains together, Martha. Either one or the other."

Aunt Martha put down the teapot. "What did you mar[ry] me for?"

His eyes were reminiscent. "Glamor, curves," he sa[id] "Boy, when you walked out on the stage with tights o[n] you—"

"So," she blazed indignantly, "*now* you're trying to te[ll] me I haven't any brains!"

Uncle Benedict shook his head. "Arguing with a woma[n]

he said, "is like trying to order the weather to suit the farmers. Where are you going in such a rush, Peggy?"

Peggy was dashing for the door. "I'm not going, I'm gone. . . ."

Peggy felt a surge of triumph when within less than an hour from the time she reached the beach city she had located the motel. The proprietress was reluctant to discuss registrations.

"We're running a decent, clean, respectable place," she said. "Of course, we don't ask people to show us marriage licenses every time they come in, but they don't do that even in the Waldorf-Astoria. We just try to look 'em over and—"

Peggy patiently interrupted to explain that hers was a private matter; that if necessary she could get official authority, but that she didn't want to and she didn't think the woman wanted her to.

That secured instant results. Peggy examined the weekend registration.

The car was 5N20861, registered to Peter Bushnell. Mr. and Mrs. Bushnell had spent the weekend in a cabin.

Peggy could have cried with disappointment. All her hopes were dashed. If she could have proved that Stella had had a boy friend with whom she had spent the weekend, then Stella's date with Don Kimberly would have looked like a mere business date. But now that had been swept away. Stella had spent the weekend with the Bushnells.

Fighting back tears, Peggy started back to her apartment. Then a thought struck her with the force of a blow. She felt certain Mrs. Bushnell had said that Pete was "still" married to her. Did that mean—?

Peggy frantically consulted the address she had taken from the registration book at the motel. It was a ten-to-one shot, but she was taking it. Peter Bushnell was going to have an unexpected visitor.

She drove rapidly to the address, an old-fashioned, unpretentious, comfortable-looking apartment house.

A card in the mailbox told her Peter Bushnell's apartment was on the second floor. Peggy didn't even stop for the elevator, but raced up the stairs to the apartment. A slender ribbon of illumination showed from the underside of the door.

Her heart hammering with excitement, she rang the bell.

Peggy heard a chair being pushed back, and then the door opened and Peggy found herself looking at the face of the man in the photograph. Now it was a haggard face, drawn with suffering.

"You're Peter Bushnell," she said. "I'm Peggy Castle. I want to talk with you."

She stepped past him into the apartment, turned, smiled reassuringly, and waited for him to close the door.

"Won't you—won't you sit down?" he said. "It's rather late, but—"

"I wanted to talk with you about Stella," she said.

His face showed consternation. "I—I have nothing to say."

"Oh, yes, you have. I know some of the facts. In justice to yourself and in justice to Stella's memory you'll have to give me the rest of them."

"What facts?"

"For instance, the weekend at the Seaswept Motel. You registered under your own name. Why did you do that, Pete?"

"Why not? The car's registered in my name. Why shouldn't I have used it?"

"Because you registered Stella as your wife."

"Well—so what?"

"Suppose Frances found out about it?"

"How would she find out?"

"I found out about it."

"How?"

Peggy merely smiled. She said, "Tell me about Stella, Pete."

"Who are you anyway?"

"I'm an investigator."

"With the police?"

"No. I represent the company Stella worked for. You don't want Stella's name dragged through the mud, and we

172

n't want it dragged through the mud. You were in love
ith her, weren't you, Pete?"

He nodded. His face showed anguish.

"Now, then, let's get down to brass tacks," Peggy said.
You married Frances. Stella was going with Bill Everett.
ou went on weekend parties together, didn't you?"

He said, "That was before I was married to Frances.
hen Fran and I got married and—well, I found out it was
mistake before we'd been married three months."

"Why was it a mistake, Pete?"

"Because I had been in love with Stella all the time and
adn't realized it. You have no idea what it was like to be
at with Stella. She was such good company. She never
alked, never got mad, never complained. She took every-
ing just the way it came, and she always had such a good
me that you had a good time too. She enjoyed life. She got
kick out of everything.

"Fran was just the opposite. Fran had to have things just
. When she was with a foursome she hid behind Stella's
ood nature so you didn't see her real character. After we
ere married and it was just the two of us—well, it showed
then."

"What happened?"

"I wanted a divorce, and Fran wouldn't give me one. She
new by that time I was in love with Stella and did every-
ing she could to block us. She swore that if she couldn't
ave me, Stella couldn't."

"So you and Frances separated, and you and Stella
arted living together?"

"Well, in a way. Not quite like that."

"Why didn't you live together all the time, Pete? Why
ose surreptitious weekends?"

"Stella was afraid of Fran. She didn't want Fran to find
out, but—well, in a way we were married."

"What do you mean?"

"We went down to Mexico and had a marriage ceremony
rformed."

"When?"

"Four or five months ago."

"Why didn't you tell the police about this?"

"Well, I was trying to make up my mind. That's what was doing when you rang the bell. I don't know what to d Fran, of course, would have me right where she wante me, but under the circumstances—I just don't know.

"Fran can be a bearcat. She's been married before. Th man she was married to wrote me a letter. He said Fra was poison, that she wouldn't give *him* a divorce, that sl was a dog in the manger."

"What did you do?"

"I hunted him out and beat him up."

Peggy, looking at the anguished face, was thinkir rapidly. There had to be an angle—there had to be!

"You knew Stella was going to have a baby?"

"Yes. Our baby. She'd only just found out herself. Sl told me Saturday."

Meeting his eyes, Peggy said, "Pete, she really *was* yo wife. Your marriage to Fran was illegal. Fran had nev been divorced."

"She told me she'd been divorced."

"Did you check on it?"

"No, I took her word for it."

"You were married to Stella, in Mexico. That marria; was legal. Stella was your legal wife. Now tell me abo Bill Everett."

"That crook! He ran with a gang. They all got caught that stickup in Cofferville."

"Had he been in touch with Stella recently?"

"Not that I know of. Not since he got out of prison."

"You haven't seen him?"

Pete shook his head.

"Did you know Stella had asked Don Kimberly to me her at the Royal Pheasant?"

"No, I didn't. She didn't say anything."

"Do you know where Bill Everett is?"

"No."

"You have no idea how I could locate him?"

"No."

"How long had he been mixed up with the gang, Pe Was it just one slip or—"

"One slip, nothing," Pete said. "The guy was just no go

right from the start. He'd been lying to us all the time. That's the way he was making his money—he was a member of a stickup gang. He thought he was smart, thought he was beating the law."

"Do you know the other members of the gang?"

He shook his head. "Guess you could find out who they were from the court records. They were all caught on that service-station stickup."

"They'd been working together for some time?"

"Apparently so," Pete said. "I don't know too much about it. Anyway, I'm all broken up. I can't think good."

Peggy said, "Try and think. Tell me everything you know about Bill."

Pete said, "The gang used to communicate with each other by ads in the personal column of a newspaper. Bill told me that once. They'd arrange meeting places and things of that sort. That's all I know."

Peggy said, "Pete, I want you to do *exactly* what I am going to tell you."

"What?" he asked.

"This," she said, "is the way to clear the thing up, provided you do *exactly* as I tell you. I want you to go down to the morgue and claim the body of Stella Lynn. Claim the body as that of your wife. Do you understand? *You're her husband.*"

"But," he said, "our marriage—well, you know, it wasn't—"

"How do you *know* it wasn't? You have Stella's memory to think of. Do exactly as I tell you. Go down to the morgue at once. Claim the body on the ground that you're Stella's husband. Don't let *anyone* get you to admit that there's even the faintest doubt in your mind about the validity of that Mexican marriage. Do you understand?"

He nodded.

"Do you have any money?" she asked.

"Enough."

"I can help—"

"No. This is on me," he said. As he pushed back his chair his manner showed the relief of one who has had a load lifted from his shoulders. . .

In the newspaper office Peggy consulted the back files, carefully scanning the Want Ad section.

In a paper of four days before she found the ad in the personal column:

"Fran, get in touch with me on a big deal. I can't handle it alone, but together we can make big dough. Call Essex 4-6810 any time day or night. Bill E."

Pieces of the jigsaw puzzle were beginning to fall into place in Peggy's mind. The next question was whether she should pour her story into the ears of Detective Fred Nelson or get some additional evidence.

A silver dime was to determine Peggy's next course. She called Essex 4-6810 and waited, her pulses pounding with excitement.

If things went through without a hitch now, she'd handle it herself. If she struck a snag over the telephone, her next call would be to Detective Nelson.

At length a masculine voice, wary, uncordial, said, "Yeah?"

"Is Bill Everett there?"

"Who wants him?"

"A girl."

The man laughed and said, "You could have fooled me."

She heard his voice raised in a call. "Bill in there? Some dame wants him on the phone."

A moment later she heard steps approaching the phone; another voice, cold, guarded but curious, said, "Yes? Hello."

"Bill?"

"Who is it?"

"I'm a friend of Fran's. It's about a butterfly."

The voice at the other end of the line instantly lost all coldness and reserve.

"Well, it's about time!" he exclaimed. "Where the hell *is* Fran? Why didn't she call me about the insurance interview?"

"She's where she can't call."

"Good Lord, you don't mean she's—"

"Now, take it easy," Peggy said. "I have a message for you."

"What is it?"

176

"Don't be silly. I can't give it to you over the phone. Where can I meet you?"

"You got a car?"

"Yes."

"Come on out here."

"Now, wait a minute," Peggy said. "There's a lot of this I didn't get from Fran. She only gave me the number to call and—"

"Adams and Elmore," he said. "It's on the corner. What kind of a car are you driving?"

"Green coupe."

"How long will it take you?"

"About fifteen minutes."

"Okay, okay, get out here! Park your bus on Elmore just before you get to Adams—on the right-hand side of the street, headed south. Sit there and wait for me. Got that?"

"Yes."

"Now, when is Fran going to—"

"Wait until I see you," Peggy interrupted. "You talk too much over the phone."

"Damned if I don't," Everett said, and she could hear the receiver being slammed into place at the other end.

Peggy then dialed police headquarters, asked for Detective Fred Nelson, and was lucky enough to find him in.

"This is Peggy Castle," she said.

"Oh, yes, hello." His voice was more cordial than she had expected.

"I have a lead on the Stella Lynn case."

"Yeah, I know," Nelson said. "You have lots of leads. You pulled the trigger on a lot of publicity, didn't you?"

"Why, what do you mean?"

"Nice and dramatic," he said. "It worked out a thousand percent. Grief-crazed husband stumbles into the morgue, tearfully claims the body of Stella Lynn, his wife. How the newspapers fell for that one! They just called me from the morgue."

He stopped talking, and Peggy said nothing.

"You there?" he asked.

"Yes."

"Well, why don't you say something?"

"You're doing the talking. I called you up to tell you something. When you get ready to listen let me know."

He laughed. "All right, I'll listen, but don't think I was born yesterday just because you didn't meet me until today. I've been around a while."

"I'm quite certain you have," Peggy said. "As I said, I have a lead in the Lynn case."

"What is it this time?"

Peggy said, "Stella wanted Don Kimberly to meet her at the Royal Pheasant because she wanted to find out if it would be possible to negotiate for the return of the gems on that Garrison job."

"What!" Nelson exclaimed.

Peggy said, "Bill Everett, Stella's ex-boy friend, was mixed up in that job. Now he's got a fortune in gems and can't fence them. You know what happens at a time like that. He wants to know whether he can make a deal with the insurance company."

"Who's this fellow you say pulled the job?"

"Bill Everett. He's been in trouble before. He was picked up in Cofferville for the robbery of a service station."

"Uh-huh, go ahead."

"I have a date with him. He's going to give me the low-down. Now, if you wanted to cooperate—"

"I'm sorry, Miss Castle," Nelson said. "You're out of bounds. Cooperating with you doesn't do anything except get your company off the hot stove and leave the Police Department holding the bag. If you have any chestnuts in the fire, just get yourself another cat's-paw."

"But don't you want to recover—"

"I want to recover from a couple of bad blows below the belt," Nelson said. "You don't know whether Bushnell was legally married to Stella Lynn or not, but you've got the story nicely planted on the front page of every newspaper, together with pictures of the stricken husband. I don't think I care about being a stalking horse. Where is this Bill Everett?"

"Find out, if you're so damned smart," she blazed, and slammed the receiver.

She drove rapidly to Elmore, followed it down toward

Adams, eased the car to a stop, and waited.

Sitting there in the dark she experienced a feeling of complete loneliness. The motor of the car made sharp crackling noises as the metal cooled off. Five blocks behind her was a through highway. The sound of traffic, muted by distance, came to her ears.

A man walked by but seemed to take no notice of the car. He moved rapidly, heels pounding the pavement as if he were going somewhere in a hurry.

Peggy waited another five minutes. Suddenly she was conscious of a shadow at the right-rear fender of the car. Then the door on the right-hand side swung open. A man eased into the seat beside her and said, "Okay, wind her up."

Peggy asked, "Are you—"

"Wind her up, I said," the man told her. "Get the hell out of here."

Peggy started the motor and glided away from the curb. The man at her side swung around so he could look through the rear window, and carefully watched the street behind him.

"Turn right on Adams," he said.

Peggy turned right.

"Left at the next intersection."

Peggy followed instructions.

"Pick up a little speed," he told her. "Don't dawdle along. All right, now give it the gun and turn right at the next intersection. . . . Okay, left again. . . . Okay."

At length the man eased back into a more comfortable position, ceased watching the road behind them, and fastened his eyes on Peggy.

Peggy was conscious of a distinct feeling of disquiet, a peculiar apprehension. Suppose everything *didn't* go right. Suppose. . . .

"It's your dime," the man said. "Start talking."

Peggy knew she had to draw him out. So far she had got by on bluff and surmise. Now she was going to need facts, and the man beside her was the only person from whom she could get those facts.

The man continued, "What's the pitch? Let's see who you

are first. I'm Bill. Who are you?"

Peggy slipped her hand down the opening of her blouse, brought out the jeweled butterfly, held it so he could see it for a brief instant, then popped it back into her blouse.

"Hey, wait a minute," he said, "where the hell did you get that?"

"Where do you suppose?"

"Here, pull into this next alley," Bill said. "We're going to have a showdown on this."

She felt something prodding at her side, and, glancing down, saw the glint of light on blued steel.

"Get over there. Turn down that alley." His shoe crushed her foot against the brake pedal.

With a little cry of pain she jerked her foot away. The car swerved. The gun jabbed hard into her ribs. "Turn down that alley!"

She bit her lip, fighting back the pain in her foot, and turned down the alley.

Bill reached over and turned off the ignition switch. "Now, baby," he said, "if you're trying to pull a fast one, what's going to happen to you isn't—"

Abruptly the car was flooded with brilliance as a following car, running without lights, suddenly blazed its headlights on the parked car.

Bill shoved the gun under his coat. "If that's a prowl car," he warned, "and you make a squawk, I'll kill you just as sure as—"

A figure jumped out of the car behind and came striding forward. A man's sneering voice said, "Well, Bill, trying to cut yourself a piece of cake, eh?"

At the sound of that voice Peggy could see Bill's face twist in a spasm of fear. He jerked his body around. "Butch!" he exclaimed, and then after a moment added, "Am I glad *you're* here! I've caught a dame trying to pull a fast one on us."

"Yeah. You look as though you're glad to see us," Butch said.

Another man came up on the other side of the car and stood at the open window on Peggy's side. He was a tall cadaverous man with lips so thin that his mouth looked as though it might have been cut across his face with a razor blade.

The man Bill had addressed as Butch said, "Get in and take the wheel, Slim. Drive up to Bill's place. Bill, you get in with us. I want to talk with you."

Slim opened the door and slapped Peggy's thigh with the back of his hand. "Move over, cutie."

Butch opened the door on the right-hand side. "Come on, Bill."

Bill said, "Sure, sure." His voice was too full of cordiality. "I want to talk things over with you guys, but listen, I think this babe is maybe a private dick or something. She's trying to pull a fast one."

"Yeah," Butch said. "We know all about this babe. Come on, get in, Bill. We're going to take a nice little ride and have a nice little talk."

Bill got out of the car. Peggy slid over on the seat, and Slim took the wheel.

"You'll have to back out," Butch said to Slim. "It's a blind alley."

"Okay."

"You take the lead," Butch went on. "If she makes any trouble, bean her." Butch moved away with Bill.

Slim reached into his side coat pocket, pulled out a blackjack, and looped the thong around his wrist. "Let's not have any misunderstanding, sister," he said. "One peep out of you, one false move, and I'll knock you so cold it'll be next week before you come to. I'm going to be driving with one hand. This other one is ready to chop you down whenever you make a yip. Get me?"

She smiled at him and said, "Aren't you making a mountain out of a molehill? Perhaps if you'll tell me—"

"Yeah, I know," Slim said, "pulling the old sex charm. It doesn't work, babe. When I'm on a business deal I'm cold as a cucumber. Now, turn your kisser around here so I can take a little precaution against any sudden screams."

"What do you mean?"

He grabbed her around the shoulders and pulled her head over to him roughly. She felt the slap of a hand across her mouth and something sticky against her cheeks. Almost before she understood what he was doing, a wide strip of adhesive tape had been slapped across her mouth. Slim's cigarette-stained fingers massaged the tape firmly into place.

"All right, baby," he said. "Don't try to raise your hands to the adhesive tape. The minute you do, you get clouted. Don't make any grabs for the steering wheel. Don't try anything funny. If you reach for the door handle you'll never know what hit you. Okay, here we go."

He drove skillfully with his left hand, his right on the back of the seat, the blackjack ready. The glint in his eyes told Peggy he was, as he had said, cold as a cucumber when he was on a business deal.

Slim tooled the car along until they glided to the curb in front of an apartment house a block from Adams and Elmore.

"Just sit still," Slim cautioned.

The other car parked behind them. Peggy saw Butch escorting Bill Everett, saw that Bill was talking volubly, rapidly, that Butch wasn't even listening.

A third man came up to address Slim briefly. "I'll go ahead and make sure the coast is clear," he said. "Wait for my flash."

"Okay," Slim said.

Bill and Butch moved into the apartment house. A light came on in a ground-floor window. The curtain was promptly drawn, shutting off the light.

A few seconds later a flashlight blinked twice.

"Okay, babe," Slim said. "Let's go."

He reached across her, opened the door, and shoved her out. She looked desperately up and down the deserted street.

Slim's hand moved deftly down her arm, caught her wrist, doubled it back until excruciating pain caused her to take a step forward to ease the pressure.

Slim stepped forward with her. The pressure remained the same.

Peggy tried to scream, but only a little whimpering noise came from behind the adhesive tape. In the end she was all but running, trying to keep just enough ahead of Slim to ease the pressure on her wrist.

She was hurried along a dark corridor. The third man, who had evidently been driving the other car, jerked open a door. Peggy was pushed inside.

Slim tossed her purse at Butch. "Catch," he said.

Butch opened her purse and examined her driving license and identification.

"Honest, Butch," Bill said, "this is a new one on me. She made contact and—"

Butch looked up from Peggy's driving license. "Shut him up, Slim."

"Okay," Slim said, moving forward.

Bill said, "No, no, I am on the level with this. She—"

Slim swung the blackjack with a deft wrist motion. The peculiar *thunk* sounded as though someone had slapped an open palm against a ripe watermelon. Bill turned glassy-eyed, his head dropped forward, he slumped down in the chair, and then, with fear in his eyes he held onto a thin margin of consciousness.

"No, no," he screamed. "You guys aren't going to do that to me!"

The peculiar *thunk* was repeated.

Butch didn't even glance at Bill. He looked at Peggy and said, "So you're from the insurance company that has the two-hundred-and-fifty-thousand-dollar policy on the Garrison gems."

Peggy pointed toward the strip of adhesive tape on her lips.

"You don't need to have that off to nod," Butch said, his eyes cold.

She remained stiff-necked, defiant. Butch jerked his head, and Slim moved over beside her.

"When I ask questions," Butch said, "I want you to answer them. Slim plays rough, and he doesn't have any more feeling about women than a snake. Now, as I get it, you work for the insurance company, and Bill was making a deal with you to turn back the gems provided you could buy him immunity and pay him maybe thirty or forty thousand bucks. Is that the case?"

She shook her head.

"Soften her up, Slim," Butch said. "She's lying."

Slim tapped the back of her neck with the blackjack. It was only a gentle tap, but it sent a sharp pain shooting through Peggy's brain. She saw a succession of bright flashes in front of her eyes and felt a numbing paralysis that gradually gave place to a dull throbbing ache.

"I'm waiting for an answer," Butch said.

She took a deep breath, fought back the nauseating headache, then shook her head determinedly.

Slim cocked his wrist and then held it at a sign from Butch, whose slightly puzzled eyes held a glint of admiration. "Damn it," he said, "the babe's got nerve!"

Butch turned to regard the unconscious Bill. Then he said, "When he comes back to join us we'll ask *him* some questions. I sure had a straight tip that Bill was in on a sellout, and—hell, it *has* to be true."

"Want me to take the tape off?" Slim asked.

"Not yet," Butch said. "We've got all night. We—"

There was a peculiar sound at the door of the apartment, a rustling noise as though garments were brushing against it.

Butch looked at Slim who moved toward the door. His right hand streaked for the left lapel of his coat, but the blackjack that was looped around the wrist impeded the motion. The door banged open explosively, hitting the wall.

Detective Fred Nelson, looking over the sights of a .38, sized up the situation. "Okay, you punks," he said, "that'll be about all."

He looked at Peggy, sitting there with the strip of tape across her lips. "I guess this time you *were* on the up and up," he said. "You got sore and wouldn't tell me where Bill Everett was living, but it happened one of the boys had done a routine check job on him because he is an ex-con.

"Now you guys line up against that wall, and keep your hands up. You can spend the night in a cell or on a marble slab, and it don't make a damn bit of difference to me which it is."

Peggy sat in Detective Fred Nelson's office. Police Captain Farwell, whose eyes made no attempt to conceal respectful admiration, sat at one end of the big table. Don Kimberly sat at the other end. Nelson asked the questions.

Peggy felt like a tightrope walker, giving them step-by-step conclusions to get Kimberly off the hook of the murder charge; but she was faced with the necessity of glossing over certain clues that she and Kimberly had suppressed and of minimizing the clues Nelson had overlooked. There was no use in making Nelson look dumb before his superior.

"A woman," Peggy explained, "naturally notices certain things a man would never see."

"What things?" Nelson asked.

"Well, for instance, a matter of housekeeping."

"Go ahead," the Captain said.

"Well," Peggy went on, choosing her words carefully, "you have to put yourself in the position of a murderer in order to understand how a murder is committed."

Captain Farwell glanced at Detective Nelson. "It isn't going to hurt you to listen to this with *both* ears," he said.

Peggy said, "Let's suppose I wanted to murder Stella Lynn by giving her a drink of poisoned whiskey. I'd have to make certain *she* drank the whiskey and I didn't. So *I'd* poison my bottle of liquor and then go call on Stella so I could get rid of her liquor.

"Now, Stella might be fresh out of whiskey, or she might have a bottle that was half full or she might have a full bottle. She was going out on a date. She wouldn't want to drink too much, and, of course, I wouldn't want to drink much because I couldn't afford to be drunk."

"So what *would* you do?" Nelson asked, his eyes still cautious.

"Why," Peggy said, "I'd make it a point to smash her bottle of whiskey so I'd have a good excuse to go out and get another one to take its place. Then I'd want to be sure Stella was the *only one* who drank out of that new bottle."

"Go ahead," the Captain said.

"Well, if you dropped the bottle on the living-room carpet, or on the kitchen floor, which had linoleum, it might not break, and then your murder plan would be out the window. There was only one place you could drop it—on

185

the bathroom tiles.

"A man would have a lot of trouble working out a scheme by which he could take the bottle of liquor Stella had, carry it into the bathroom, and drop it—without the whole business seeming very strange. But a *woman* could do it easily.

"She'd run in while Stella was dressing. Stella would say to her, 'I'm getting ready to go out on a date, but come in and talk to me anyway,' and the woman would have all the chance in the world to carry the liquor to the bathroom, start to pour a drink, drop the bottle, and say, 'Oh, dear, Stella. I've dropped your whiskey. You go right ahead with your dressing. I'll run down, get another bottle, and then clean up this mess.'

"So the woman went to get the other bottle of whiskey— the bottle that had been poisoned and then resealed. She came back with the package, handed it to Stella, and said, 'Now, Stella, you just go right ahead with your dressing and I'll clean up this mess in the bathroom.'

"So she started picking up the pieces of glass, and Stella took the new bottle of whiskey. Stella being Stella, she simply had to open it, pour herself a good-sized drink, and toss it off."

There was silence for several seconds, then Captain Farwell nodded slowly and again glanced at Nelson.

Nelson said almost defensively, "It's a damned good theory, but where's the proof?"

"The proof," Peggy said, her eyes wide and innocent, "why, there's *plenty* of proof. I looked carefully at the bathroom floor to see if there weren't little pieces of glass that hadn't been cleaned up. It's awfully hard to clean up glass slivers, you know. Sure enough, there were several little pieces."

Nelson took a deep breath.

"Yes," he said, "we saw them."

"And then, of course, the broken bottle that was out in the trash can in the back yard. You see, the whiskey had to be mopped up, and the murderer's hands were sticky and they left a beautiful set of fingerprints on the broken bottle."

"Where's that bottle?" Captain Farwell asked.

Nelson's eyes shifted.

"Oh, Mr. Nelson has it," Peggy said quickly. "He's got *all* the evidence, and it occurred to me that if Mr. Nelson would have his men comb the neighborhood thoroughly to see if someone didn't leave a package at a nearby drug store or restaurant, or someplace around there where she could go back and get it, and they could identify that woman— Then, of course, there are the fingerprints."

"Whose fingerprints are they?" Captain Farwell asked Nelson.

Peggy answered the question. "We'll have to let Mr. Nelson finish the detail work before we know for sure, but they have to be those of Mrs. Bushnell.

"You see, we've established that Stella was killed by a woman. We know Bill Everett got Fran to try to arrange a sellout with the insurance company. His only point of contact was Frances, and her point of contact was Stella.

"And Fran was the only one who simply wouldn't have dared to take that butterfly. If she had, Bill would have known she was so jealous of Stella that she used the opportunity to kill Stella instead of peddling the gems to the insurance company.

"She wrote me that anonymous letter telling me Kimberly and Stella were going to meet at the Royal Pheasant, then planted the poison in his darkroom—"

"How did *she* know I'd suggest a meeting at the Royal Pheasant?" Kimberly asked.

"She knew that was the most natural spot. Stella had told her she'd arrange a meeting, and Fran must have figured you'd say the Royal Pheasant. If you had named some other place Fran could have tipped me off. But you didn't."

Captain Farwell got to his feet. "Well," he said, "the newspaper boys are out there yelling their heads off, wanting to get in and get some action. I don't care what the details are, just so—" He paused and looked at Peggy, then looked at Don Kimberly. "Just so the department gets the credit for doing the damned fine job that it did.

"And on this murder," Captain Farwell went on, "we're sorry, Kimberly, that we had to take you into custody."

"Oh, think nothing of it," Kimberly said.

Captain Farwell left the room.

Peggy got to her feet. "Well," she said, "we won't be here when you're talking with the newspapermen, Mr. Nelson. You can handle that. I'll get you the broken whiskey bottle with the fingerprints on it. Of course, you understand that E.B. Halsey, president of the company, is very anxious to have a good press for the insurance company—"

"Sure, sure, I understand," Nelson said, "and we want to thank you folks for your cooperation."

"I take it I'm free to walk out?" Kimberly asked.

Nelson nodded. "Hell, yes. Want me to pull out a red carpet?"

Don Kimberly looked at Peggy Castle as though suddenly seeing her for the first time.

"Come on, glamor puss," he said. "Let's go and let Nelson get his work done. You're too pretty to be mixed up in a sordid crime."

"Oh, how nice!" Peggy exclaimed. "Just wait till I tell my Uncle Benedict what you just said!"